I0570079

Names Written in Water

A Joshua MacMillan Mystery

Kerry Mack Wright

Aureum Press Atlanta

This book is a work of fiction. All characters, events, organizations, and locations portrayed in this novel are either based on the author's imagination or are used fictitiously.

First published in the United States by
Aureum Press, Atlanta, GA

Cover Art by Liz Hume
http://www.lizhumestudio.com

ISBN Print Edition: 979-8-9991064-0-7
Subjects: FIC022100 Fiction / Mystery /
Detective / Amateur Sleuth
ISBN Kindle Edition: 979-8-9991064-1-4

"Here Lies One Whose Name Was Writ in Water"

-Epitaph on the tombstone of British poet John Keats

This book is dedicated to those we
loved who were gone too soon.

PROLOGUE
July 1982

It was another hot, humid night in the Mississippi Delta, the air so thick the moon wore a hazy cowl. Even at midnight the asphalt in the alley continued to radiate heat stored from the day. A swarm of moths and bugs orbited the streetlight, transfixed by its flickering light. The incessant sawing of cicadas was interrupted only by the bug zapper when it lit up, frying its prey in purple heat.

Several cars were crammed into this small parking lot. Notable among them was a new, cream-colored convertible, its top down. Its driver-side door was standing open, as if waiting patiently and courteously for its master to come home. However, its driver was not coming home.

Ever. Again.

She lay next to the open door, crumpled on the oil and grease-stained pavement. Her short, dark hair fell away from her face, and her blue eyes were vacant and blank, staring into eternity. Her denim mini skirt rode up promiscuously, while blood bloomed like a funeral rose across her white crop top. A pool of blood grew at her back.

The back door to the bar banged open, and a cloud of cigarette smoke poured into the night. The sounds of an oldies band overpowered the noise of the cicadas until the door slammed shut. A man carrying several bags of trash strode toward the dumpster. When he saw the woman, he froze. He dropped the garbage bags, transfixed by what he saw, no longer hearing the cicadas, who claimed the night.

CHAPTER ONE
"The Kindness of Strangers"

Joshua felt relaxed, maybe for the first time in over a year. His baby blue and white VW Bus was eating up white lines as he puttered down the Delta highway. With the windows down, the wind ruffled his dark brown hair and played about his short beard. The morning sun was bright, but his Aviators kept out the glare. In the fields along the road, the cotton was June green and ankle high. He was still buzzing from watching BB King play the night before in his Beale Street club in Memphis. Joshua had B.B.'s latest cassette tape to prove it.

He had left Ashville in early June, shortly after school was out. His first stop was the 1982 World's Fair in Knoxville, where the Chinese exhibit alone made it worth the visit. Joshua was amazed by the gold artwork, figurines, jewelry, and coins; but he was awed by the terracotta soldiers. And then, there was country music super group Alabama in a pasture at Redgate Farm in nearby Luttrell, Tennessee. He next traveled to Nashville to hear some new country acts at the Blue Bird Cafe, but his Nashville highlight was seeing Johnny Cash with the Carter Family at the Ryman Auditorium. And then, it was on to Memphis for BB.

Not a bad road trip so far.

And now he was headed to New Orleans to hear more live music at the legendary Warehouse. After that, he planned to travel along the coast to Orange Beach, Alabama to visit the famous Flora-Bama bar, where hopefully he would hear Jimmy Buffet play.

The news on NPR this warm, Mississippi morning was all about the Peace Rally at Central Park in New York. 750,000 people attended a rally against nuclear weapons; and Jackson Browne, Linda Ronstadt, Bruce Springsteen, and James Taylor were there. Maybe there was some hope for this world after all, Joshua thought. Tired of the news, he was ready to hear his new BB King tape, so he punched it in. "The Thrill Is Gone" wailed from his stereo speakers.

The song was only halfway over when a loud clang erupted from the engine, followed by the screech of grinding metal. The bus lurched violently, but Joshua had the presence of mind to pop the clutch, so he was able to coast to the shoulder of the road. Climbing out of the driver's seat, he went to the back of his vehicle and propped open the engine compartment. No smoke or anything like that. That was good. But....

"Please don't tell me I've thrown a rod!" he shouted to the cotton fields.

He looked north along the shimmering road, flat and empty for miles, and then he looked south. Nothing but miles and miles of nothing but miles and miles. To Joshua, who hailed from the hills of North Carolina, the Delta was like an alien world. It was so flat and the horizon so very big. Nothing to do but begin to walk. He was soaked with sweat before he saw the first sign: "Indian Springs - 6 Miles."

The thrill was definitely gone.

Finally, he heard a vehicle coming, so he stuck out his thumb. The rusty pickup slowed to a stop, and the driver rolled down his window.

"You need some hep?"

"A ride into town would be great!"

"Git in!"

Fifteen minutes later, the Good Samaritan let him out in front of Joe's Garage at the western edge of Indian Springs. The bay door was open, and a big fan was working hard against the heat.

"Hello!" Joshua called out.

"Be with you in a minute." A tall, lanky black man with a lined face and wooly white hair emerged from the back, wiping his hands on a red grease towel. "What can I do for ya'?"

Joshua introduced himself and said, "Yes, sir. My car broke

down about eight miles outside of town. Is there any way you could tow it in and check it out? I'm afraid it may have thrown a rod."

"What make and model?"

"1969 Volkswagen Bus."

The old man shook his head doubtfully. "I can tow it in, but nobody around here works on Volkswagens that I know of. If you threw a rod, that means a new engine, or at least, a good used one. That might take a while to find, and I would need help to install it. Those VW's were made for colder weather, like in northern Europe. They don't do so well in this heat and humidity, especially with those air-cooled engines." Not the news Joshua wanted to hear, but at least it was a start.

"OK. When can we go get it?"

"Let me fix you a glass of ice water. You cool down a bit while I finish up this oil change."

"That would be great. Thanks!"

Within a couple of hours, he and Joe had the VW towed and parked behind the garage. After Joshua paid the mechanic, he realized to his dismay that a new engine was not in his budget for his road trip to the coast. He could tow the VW home, but that long of a trip would probably cost more than the VW was worth. He thought about selling it for junk and taking a Greyhound bus home, but it made him sick to think about giving up his beloved van. He had worked so hard to restore the body.

"So, you think you can find me an engine, Mr. Joe?"

"Well, I can try. I can call some folks I know down in Jackson and have them look around, but I expect a used engine and installation could cost you around $500."

For the first time, Joshua fully grasped his predicament. That much money was equal to ten weeks of groceries for a guy like him who brought home less than $7,000 a year. He did not have the money to get his bus fixed, and he still had his rent and so forth to pay back home. Would it be possible to get a job here to make the extra money? But where would he stay in the meantime? And that would mean paying rent in two places.

Joshua said, "Well, I'll check back with you, if that's OK. Are you alright with my VW sitting out back, in the meantime?"

"No problem."

"Is there a motel in town you would recommend?" Joe shook his head no. "No? Why not?"

"We don't have one," Joe said.

Joshua's face reddened. "I might wind up having to sleep in the back seat of my VW tonight, if that's not a problem."

"Well, uh, I guess you are kinda' stuck. Maybe that would be OK. For now."

With darkness quickly coming, Joshua figured he had better get some chow. On the way to Joe's, he noticed a 7-11 just around the corner. So, he set out to see what they might have. They had fried chicken and potato logs, so with a Coke and a Snickers bar, he had a meal. The good news was they had a little picnic table indoors where he could eat under the air conditioning. After he finished eating, he headed back to Joe's to settle into his VW bus.

Fortunately, the battery was good, so he was able to read under the soft glow of the interior lights. Churchill, one of his favorites. Before too long, though, his eye lids began to flutter, so he made his way to the back seat to stretch out. The problem was that it was still hot. Opening the windows helped some, and before long, he faded into sleep. He did not sleep well, however. He started awake several times to slap the buzzing mosquitoes away from his face, and he was soaked with sweat. His dreams were strange and unsettling. In them, he was hacking his way through wet, foul jungle. He was looking for someone, but he did not know where to look. She shouldn't be in the jungle; she should be in the mountains. Struggling up from his nonsensical dream, he found himself "praying for daylight."

***

The next morning, he asked Mr. Joe if he could use his bathroom, and it was there that he took a cold rag bath and changed clothes. He grabbed a cinnamon bun and coffee at the 7-11 and lingered in the air conditioning. Afterwards, with nothing better to do, he wandered into the downtown area of Indian Springs, past the old hardware store and other businesses, and down towards the square. Typical of a small Southern town, there was a Courthouse, although nondescript. There were lots of trees, magnificent magnolias in full bloom, surrounded by lush green grass and beautiful flower beds. He walked past a spacious library with Grecian style columns out front, and then he passed what looked like an old, red-brick schoolhouse. It had a daylight basement, and concrete steps led up to the first floor. As he rounded the corner, he saw a parking lot in the back. Curious, he walked around to that side of the building. It looked like maybe a pub or something was in the basement.

Joshua walked up to the door of the bar, aptly named The Boiler Room, where he saw the "Help Wanted" sign in the front window. He wondered if that might just be the answer to his money problem. If not, maybe at least they'll have cold beer, he reasoned.

As it turned out, they had both.

Surprisingly, the bar was open, probably for stocking, he figured. Walking inside, he surveyed the landscape. It was amazing what they had done to the basement and boiler room of the old high school, turning a labyrinth of connected rooms into a cool hangout. The larger area to the left was for the band on Friday and Saturday nights and any dancing that could be squeezed in among its tables and chairs. A smaller area in the back and to the left held a couple of pool tables, and another area in the back right had video games, like PacMan and Galaga, state of the art for the early 80's. The liquor-lined bar to the right, with mirror and polished wood, lent the air of a neighborhood pub, which it was during the week. The vintage bar was nestled into an alcove that had been converted from the coal room. Joshua walked over to the bar and took a seat on one of the stools.

"Uh, we're not actually open," said the pretty, statuesque bartender as she walked in, pulling back her long, ash-blonde hair. "What can I do for you?"

"What I really need is a job."

"Oh, so you saw the sign?" she said. The bartender narrowed her green eyes as she sized him up. Hiking boots, Levi's, and a B.B. King t-shirt; tall and lean; nice blue eyes. And a wedding band on his finger.

"Yes. What are you looking for?"

"We need an experienced bartender."

"Oh, I'm your man, then. I worked my way through college tending bar."

"OK, well I can test your knowledge later, but for now, what's your name?"

"Joshua. Joshua MacMillan."

"My name is Sabrina Goodman," she said with a smile. "I don't recognize your name. Do you live around here?"

"No, I'm actually from North Carolina. I'm on summer break, so I WAS taking a road trip." He explained about his bus breaking down and the need for a job.

"Ah, the intriguing stranger!" Sabrina said with a grin and a wink of her eye, but Joshua missed the humor. She noticed a hint of sadness about him, something beyond a broken-down car and the need for a job. Her heart went out to him. And that ring. What was he doing on a road trip by himself if he was married?

"Well, you would fit right in at The Boiler Room. It's like the 'it' hangout for non-natives. I'm not from here, either, and I can tell you first-hand that if you're not from here, you might as well be from Mars. There are several people who have moved here from other places for work, but the only friends this town will let them make are other outsiders. And The Boiler Room is just the place to make them."

"Believe me, I know this kind of town. The one I came from is just like it."

"We have something in common, then. What kind of work do you do in North Carolina that gives you a summer break? Wait, let me guess. Are you a teacher by any chance?"

"Yes. High school history, but I also help a friend in his bar on the weekends when he needs me."

"Great! Give me some numbers to call for references, and if that works out, I'll give you a shot. Oh, there will still be a 'bar exam,'" she said and chuckled at her own joke.

***

Sabrina confirmed Joshua's employment with his school district, and she got solid references from a couple of former bar managers. On top of that, he was able to pass Sabrina's "bar exam" with flying colors, so he was hired.

The Boiler Room proved to be a good place to work for a guy like him. "Things 'er heatin' up at The Boiler Room!" was their corny advertising slogan, but in reality, the place was mostly a cozy little pub. The jukebox was usually playing on weeknights, and typically, a few couples could be seen slow dancing to songs like Dolly Parton and Kenny Rogers' "Islands in the Stream." Joshua learned that through a door behind the billiards area, one could connect to the dressing room of the old auditorium above. That's where the community theater held its plays. They specialized in comedies, since the extras had a hard time staying sober. The bar was close, and the wait could be long before their chance to "strut and fret their hour upon the stage." Or stumble, as the case might be.

He also learned that through a door at the end of the bar, there was an intimate, French-style restaurant named Le Monde - "The World," which was situated in what was once the school's small cafeteria. It closed before the band cranked up on Friday and Saturday nights. The restaurant had its own entrance, but it shared the bar with The Boiler Room, and in turn, it provided pub fare for thirsty patrons. Joshua would come to like their clam chowder. Made a good supper before work.

A week passed, and he got into the routine, blending well with the other non-residents like him. He still did not have an engine for his bus, however. Fortunately, his two nights of sleeping in the back seat of his VW ended when Sabrina realized his plight. As it turned out, her husband Scott was the director of the community theater, and they were rehearsing *A*

Streetcar Named Desire - not a comedy for a change. They told Joshua he was welcome to sleep in what would later become Blanche DuBois' bed, until he could find a room. As he lay in bed the first night, he realized with irony that like Blanche, he was "depending upon the kindness of strangers." It felt surreal sleeping in the musty old theater, but it was better than the cramped van in the stifling Mississippi heat. And the gym locker room's cold showers beat a rag bath from the sink in Joe's Garage. Still, those creaking noises in the night!

His second Friday night at the bar came, and he was feeling much more at home. He was getting to know some of the regulars, including two of Sabrina's friends who were police officers. Jeff and Reuben dropped by regularly when they were off duty. Always good to have friends like that in a bar. On this night, a popular oldies band was playing. Interesting group, The Mindbenders. The four musicians - base, lead, drums, and keyboard - ranged in age from 16 to 62, with the oldest sporting a long beard like one of those guys from ZZ Top. The kicked the night off with the Rolling Stones' "Jumping Jack Flash" and brought down the house.

When they went on break, the jukebox kicked in. The blend of music on that thing was hilarious. One minute it was classic Johnny Cash and "Folsom Prison Blues," and the next minute it was "Super Freak" by Rick James. "Sweet Home, Alabama" by Lynard Skynard, followed by "You Dropped the Bomb on Me" by the Gap Band.

In the meantime, the lead singer's young wife came up to the bar. "You're new here, aren't you?"

"Yep, I'm Joshua."

Flipping her mass of curly, yellow-blonde hair, she said, "Well, hey there, Joshua. Welcome to Indian Springs! I'm Carly Jane Lacy. My friends call me Carly Jane, but the boys who are interested call me Miss Carly. So, what are you going to call me?"

Joshua was taken aback, and his face showed it. She laughed and said, "I was just pulling your laig. I've got a ring on my finger just like you do."

"So, you're Carly Jane. Like Carly Simon?"

She laughed and said, "I wish I could write like her, but I'm not in her league. Besides, I'm more into Stevie Nicks."

"You look like her, too! What can I get you?"

She blushed and grinned. "Ya'll don't have what I really want, so I'll take a Jack and Coke. And I need four Bud Lights for the boys in the band."

Joshua also grinned. "Coming right up!"

He reckoned that the town and the bar were getting more and more interesting every day.

CHAPTER TWO
"All the World's a Stage"

The next week, Sabrina and her husband Scott invited Joshua over for lunch on Tuesday. They lived in an apartment that was part of an older home a few blocks from the bar. Since Scott was from Louisiana, he had a way with Cajun food. Thus, Sabrina told Joshua they would serve red beans and rice and seafood gumbo, with Tarte a' la Bouille, also known as Cajun Custard Pie, for dessert. Sounded great to him.

When he knocked on the door, Scott answered it. Joshua did a double take. Scott could have passed as Peter Fonda's character in *Easy Rider*, replete with well-trimmed, mutton chop sideburns and Ray-Ban Olympian style glasses. He introduced himself, motioning for Joshua to come in. Sabrina and Scott also invited a couple of the theater regulars, hoping that Joshua would get to know some of the other "outsiders." Motioning to the couple, Scott introduced them as Greg and Shelly Jensen.

Before long, lunch was ready, and they sat down to eat. Scott knew this cuisine well. Everyone chimed in on how good the food tasted, especially the gumbo. At one point, all that could be heard were the sounds of chewing and swallowing and spoons clashing with bowls, sometimes interrupted by the slurping of sweet tea.

As the lunch neared its conclusion, Joshua asked Scott, "What's it like being a director in community theater?"

"Well, Josh, you gotta' love it," began Scott. "We wind up moving around a lot."

Joshua winced at the nickname "Josh," but said, "So why do you move around so much?"

"Well, Josh, things will go OK for a theater group for a time, so they can afford to hire someone like me. Then, the group eventually runs low on money, and we are forced to move on. A person has to love the theater to live like this."

"I take it you do, then?" Greg asked.

"Absolutely! But if Sabrina didn't love it, it would never work, that's for sure."

"And even then..." Sabrina said sarcastically.

"What about ya'll?" Joshua said to Greg and Shelly. "You don't sound like you're from around here."

"That's right," Shelly laughed. "The famous Midwestern 'no accent' gave us away."

"Yeah, we're actually from St. Louis," Greg said. "We moved here for the job. I'm the manager of the local Mississippi Bank. We couldn't turn down the opportunity, even though it was a big change coming to the Delta. The only thing that saved us was finding a theater community."

"Greg does a lot of set work for us. He has been a godsend!" Scott said.

"And Shelly will play the role of Stella in the upcoming play," added Greg.

"What a role!" Joshua said.

"You know *Streetcar*?" Scott asked.

"Uh, I know someone who loved it," he answered wistfully. "I look forward to seeing it."

Scott and Sabrina exchanged puzzled glances at his response.

With the delicious meal over, Joshua reflected that it was good to make new friends, especially some who were outsiders like himself. The home-cooking was amazing, but relaxing in someone's home was a blessing. He hoped to find something for himself soon.

***

Fortunately for Joshua, he worked late, so his "sleeping quarters" were available after play practice. On some nights, the cast of *Streetcar* would come down to decompress when they were done. One night, Scott, the Jensen's, and some other cast members and crew came down. One cast member caught his eye.

She was the first to burst through the dressing room door and the first to reach the bar. She had short dark hair and blue eyes, and she wore a short, blue jean skirt. She was a cutie, and she knew it.

"Well, hey there," she said, speaking to him. "You must be new here. What's your name?" He told her and she said, "Well, Joshua, you're looking mighty fine tonight. How 'bout a shot of Jose and a Lite beer to chase it with." Placing the beer on a coaster and the shot on the bar, he smiled. The woman quickly downed the shot and took a long swig of the beer.

"Hooo! There you go! Thank you so much, sugar! By the way, my name's Dee Dee, and you WILL be seeing me again," she said with a wink. Turning from the bar, she sashayed to the jukebox, put a quarter in, and began to dance by herself to "Looking for Love in All the Wrong Places." Joshua found himself staring after her.

Sabrina walked over and poked him, grinning and nodding toward the woman. "So, you find her attractive?" she asked.

"Aah. Not really. Cute, yes. Attractive, no."

"Riiiiight!"

"C'mon, Sabrina. She's not my type."

"Oh, you have a type?"

"You know what I mean. She is cute, but she just seems so, I don't know.... All her flirting just seems so sad in a way."

Sabrina huffed, wondering again about the ring on his finger.

"She said her name is Dee Dee?"

"Yes, the infamous Dee Dee Scarborough. Mama's, hide your husbands!"

"So, what's up with her?" he asked, as he dried a set of glasses fresh from the dishwasher.

"She's the biggest tease in town. Before tonight's over, she will dance with every young guy in the bar, including you, if you let her. She's married to Paul Scarborough, the big boss at the refinery. He's quite a bit older, and quite a bit more well-off."

"She's married?" he asked, arching an eyebrow.

"Yep. Hard to tell, right?"

Dee Dee danced over to Scott and coaxed him onto the floor. Joshua could feel Sabrina's hackles rising. When the music changed to "Open Arms" by Journey, Dee Dee pulled him close, beginning a slow dance. Sabrina's face reddened, and she marched off through the bar door into the restaurant. With the song over, Dee Dee came back over to the bar.

"Give me another shot and another Lite beer, sweet thing."

"Yes, ma'am."

"Don't 'ma'am' me, I'm no older than you!"

Downing the shot and swilling the beer, she teased, "Wanna' come have a dance with me?"

"Thanks, but I can't leave the bar area."

"Is Sabrina spoiling all your fun?"

"Nah. There's a time and a place, that's all."

"Well, you just let me know the time, and I'll find the place," she said with a wink, as she sauntered away.

"Lor-dee!" Joshua muttered, shaking his head.

Sabrina returned from the restaurant, the color on her cheeks somewhat back to normal.

"You alright?" he asked.

"Yeah, it's just that Dee Dee really gets under my skin. She needs to go home to her man and leave mine alone."

"Wait, she came down with the cast. What part does she play in *Streetcar*?"

"Blanche DuBois, of course. Definitely typecast. She doesn't EVEN have to act for that role."

***

A week before opening night, the set was finished. Thus, Joshua made the move from Blanche DuBois' bed to a blow-up mattress on Shelley and Greg's living room floor. Scott was in an almost manic state as they prepared to open the show. The troupe planned to perform *Streetcar* on Thursday, Friday, and Saturday night at 7 PM with a Sunday afternoon matinee at 3. Joshua would handle "Thirsty Thursday," so Sabrina could attend the premier with Scott. Then, the two bartenders would work side-by-side on the busy Friday and Saturday nights. They did not schedule a band, to hold down the noise, but Le Monde did offer a dinner theater special. Since the bar was closed on Sundays, Joshua would be able to attend the matinee, and they could host the after-party at The Boiler Room.

He was looking forward to seeing the sets that Greg Jensen designed, and he was interested to see how Greg's wife Shelly handled the role of Stella. And of course, he wondered about Dee Dee as Blanche. The person he had not met was the fellow playing the role of Stanley Kowalski. He looked forward to seeing his performance and meeting him. After the show's opening night, Sabrina and Scott came down to the bar.

"How did it go, Scott?" Joshua asked.

"Don't get him started," said Sabrina. "He will tell you every little thing that went wrong."

"No, I won't!"

Sabrina continued, "The show was actually pretty good overall, especially for opening night. As Scott can tell you, the second night is usually much better."

"Yes, and then on the third night, it is terrible because everyone is tired."

"Yes, Scott, but then on Sunday, everyone gives it their best shot to finish up."

"True," Scott admitted, "but tonight was rougher than I wanted. Honestly, between us, Shelly Jensen struggled a little bit."

"Well, that is a tough role," Sabrina put in.

"Well, yeah, honestly it is. She has to pull off loyalty to both her sister and her husband, as well as the earthiness required of her relationship with Stanley."

"As they say, 'it is what it is,'" Sabrina said. "Don't be so negative."

"It's just that we have worked so hard."

"Honey, it shows," said Sabrina, putting her arm around Scott.

"Well, how was Dee Dee?" Joshua asked.

"Spectacular, as always," the director gushed. Sabrina rolled her eyes.

"What was the crowd like?" Joshua asked.

"Well, that's the best part," said Scott, cheering up somewhat. "It was really good for a Thursday night. If our crowd tomorrow is a usual Friday night crowd, we should make money on the show."

"That's great! How did the audience respond?"

"My after-show spies said that the crowd was bubbling with excitement and approval."

"See, don't be negative, honey!" Sabrina said.

Scott grinned and gave Sabrina a look as if to say, enough already! I get it!

***

The show closed on Sunday afternoon, and it was an unqualified success. Friday night was sold out, and Saturday nearly was. Even the Sunday matinee hosted a good crowd, including Joshua. He was impressed with the local talent, and he really liked Greg's elaborate sets. Everything looked so authentic, like the pictures of New Orleans he had seen, as they employed light and sound and visuals to create a real feel for the city.

Joshua also thought that Shelly Jensen did an admirable job of playing Stella. She did not overact, nor did she overdo the Southern accent. Dee Dee was perfect as Blanche. If her life had gone a little differently, she could have had a career, he thought. And Stanley? Little could Joshua have guessed that Jeff, the police officer who was an off-duty visitor to The Boiler Room, could act! And he looked the part. He must have spent many hours working out, based on his upper body physique that he showed off in his "wife-beater." Joshua would not have recognized him if it weren't for Reuben's catcalls when Stanley first came on stage. And when he bellowed his iconic line, Jeff brought down the house. "Stell-aaaaaaahhhhhhhh!"

Time for the after-show party, which meant that he and

Sabrina went to work. While state and local law did not allow the bar to be open on Sunday, they could host a private party, if they did not sell alcohol. No problem. The Indian Springs Theater Company ordered beer and wine and had it delivered the day before. Le Monde provided appetizers, also paid for by the theater group. The entire cast was there, along with their significant others. The crew and their friends did not miss out, either.

Jeff and Reuben came up to the bar, and Jeff loudly said, "As much money as I have spent in this bar, it's about time I got a free beer!"

"You earned it!" Joshua said. "I had no idea you could act. Great job!"

"Thanks. I wouldn't have ever considered doing it, but Sabrina kept hounding me. Playing Stanley was a hoot!"

"Yeah, well, you didn't have to do too much acting to play a primitive muscle head," Reuben teased as he punched Jeff in the arm.

Greg and Shelly joined in at the bar and asked for a couple of Chardonnay's. "Shelly, you did a really good job!" Joshua said, as Sabrina poured the wine. "And Greg. Those sets! I felt like I was there in New Orleans. That must have taken a lot of work!"

"It did, but it was fun. Had a bunch of great helpers, too. Little did I know that working construction as a teen would prepare me so well for set production," he said with a laugh.

And then, as though she timed it, the star of the show appeared. Dee Dee swept into the room and up to the bar, all eyes on her. Directing her attention to Joshua, she drawled in character as Blanche, "'I have always depended upon the kindness of strain-jahs.' Hey, stranger, how about a shot of Jose and a Lite beer," she said, batting her eyelashes and grinning.

Joshua couldn't help but smile in reply, placing her drink order on the bar. She promptly downed the Jose, planted a kiss on both Jeff and Reuben's cheeks, and took her Lite beer with her to the dance area, where she began to flirt with one of the younger crew members.

Once everyone had a drink and some appetizers, it was time to make a toast. Scott did the honors. "Ladies and gentlemen, and I say that loosely, may I have your attention please," he called out to the laughing troupe. "I would like to propose a toast. Thank you to the actors, the set crew, the sound crew, the technical director, and the stagehands for all your hard work. Job well done!"

The applause was loud and long.

"Here's to you, the best community theater in the South and the best show this year! Salute!" There was a loud cheer, and everyone turned up their glass. "And now, let me remind you," Scott added, "don't get too tight. We still have to strike that set tonight. And I don't want to see anyone slinking off. 'Many hands make light work,' as they say."

"Yeah, yeah," Jeff said, smirking.

"Time for some music and dancing!" Sabrina called out and plunked down two rolls of quarters on the bar. Within seconds, "Jack and Diane" by John Cougar Mellencamp got the crowd moving.

Surveying the room, looking at his new friends, Joshua wasn't so sure he wanted to go back to North Carolina even when he got his bus fixed. There was no longer anything there for him. And to reinforce his decision, Sabrina walked over to him.

"What's the matter, Josh?" she asked. "Your date stand you up? Why don't you pick out a lovely lady and take her for a twirl around the floor? You're not on the clock today."

He looked down at his ring, his face reddening.

Sabrina realized she had said the wrong thing, somehow. "I'm sorry. No offense. I didn't mean any harm. What's wrong?"

He looked at Sabrina steadily and said, "No harm done, but that's a story for another day. Just a touchy subject. And, if you don't mind, I'd rather be called Joshua." Left unsaid was that "Josh" was a nickname given him by a special person. It stung to hear it from anyone else.

"Hold on Loosely" by 38 Special began on the jukebox, and Dee Dee grabbed Scott from behind, twirled him around, and snuggled close to dance. Joshua could almost see steam rising from Sabrina's ears.

"I have had enough of this!" Sabrina swung open the bar gate with a bang, marched over to Scott, and grabbed him by the arm. She pulled him away from Dee Dee, but not before giving her a look like death. Dee Dee shrugged her shoulders and walked away. Sabrina hauled Scott over to a corner and began to let him have it. She was gesturing wildly, and he held his arms up in surrender - or self-defense - hard to say. And then she stormed out of the door of the bar, slamming it closed with a bang.

Scott looked around helplessly for a moment and then followed her out.

Joshua knew what that meant. Scott was in big trouble. It also meant that clean-up would be all on him. "Great!" he said with a sigh.

CHAPTER THREE
"What Goes Around, Comes Around"

The house was packed the following Friday night, and Joshua and Sabrina barely had time to breathe. Even though the drink orders were simple - beer or whiskey and Coke - it was order after order, and they found themselves in a dizzying dance of movement behind the bar, weaving in and out to avoid a collision. The smell of cigarettes and spilled beer washed over them. Never could get that Friday night smell out of his clothes, Joshua reflected, no matter what he used at the laundry mat. Things slowed down a bit, and Joshua noticed that Sabrina was nowhere to be seen.

"Hmmph! I could use a break, too," he muttered.

And then, like clockwork, the band took a break, and the rush began again. Fortunately, Sabrina rejoined him behind the bar. Joshua noticed she had a strained expression on her face when she returned, however. When he had a chance, he spoke.

"Are you OK? Where were you?"

"I'm fine," Sabrina hissed, brushing him off as she slid in front of him to reach for a shot glass. After she grabbed it, she turned, and he could see her eyes. They were bloodshot, teary-eyed, and unfocused.

Wondering what happened, he said, "Are you sure you're OK?"

Sabrina stopped in her tracks. She started to speak, then stopped. Then she said shakily, "I'm sorry. I was with Scott. We had a fight."

"I'm sorry, Sabrina, if I spoke out of turn. It's really none of my business." With that, a silence ensued between the two of them, as they continued to fill drink orders.

When the next break in the action finally came, Joshua

checked the trash and saw that it needed to be taken out. With both hands grasping bags of garbage, he banged through the metal side door leading to the alley and the garbage bins. He was followed by a cloud of cigarette smoke, along with the sounds of the oldies band cranking up again. It was another hot, sticky night in the Mississippi Delta, with the heat of the day radiating from the asphalt in the alley. A swarm of moths and bugs danced around the streetlight, led by the music of buzzing cicadas. The bug zapper routinely lit up, keeping time with nature's music.

As he swung the garbage bags, humming a tune, he passed several cars crammed into the small parking lot. Near the end of the lot, he noticed a new, cream-colored convertible, its top down. Its driver-side door was standing open. The driver lay next to the open door of the convertible, crumpled on the oil and grease-stained pavement.

"What the hell!" he exclaimed, dropping the garbage bags.

It was a woman, and as he stared at her, a tremor passed through his hands. His heart began to pound, and for one horrible moment, he thought it was her – HER! - lying there. Shrugging off his shock, he rushed over to see if she needed help. Then, Joshua saw her eyes. She was dead.

He had seen death; he knew it when he saw it.

It should have been hard to tell who she was in the dim light of the distant streetlamp, but there was no mistaking Dee Dee Scarborough. He had seen her earlier at the bar, ordering tequila shots and Lite Beer, flirting with all the guys, as usual. Her short, dark hair fell away from her face, and her blue eyes were vacant and blank, staring into eternity. Her denim mini skirt rode up, while blood bloomed like a funeral rose across her white crop top. A pool of blood grew at her back.

"Better go let somebody know," he murmured. "I can't believe this! Right here at the bar!" he said, shaking his head in wonder. With that, he swung open the back door, and the blast of sound from The Mindbenders and their raucous fans once again assaulted him. "What Kind of Fool Do You Think I Am?"

the band sang. Squirming his way through the packed crowd, Joshua stared at Sabrina until she looked up from pouring a Jim Beam and Coke. He gave her a look that said, We've got trouble. Swinging open the bar gate, she followed him to a corner.

"What's going on?" Sabrina asked, looking back towards the bar.

He had to raise his voice against the din to speak. "There's a woman lying out in the alley," he said unsteadily. "She's dead." Her eyes grew wide, and a shadow passed over her face. She looked away. Joshua looked over his shoulder and then back to Sabrina. He said, "I'm serious. We need to do something."

She could see the concern in his eyes. "Do you know who it is?"

"Yeah, it's Dee Dee."

"What!? Dee Dee! She's dead? Are you sure?" Joshua nodded yes.

At that moment, two of Mississippi's finest - Jeff and Reuben - ambled in through the front door. Jeff called out, "Hey, Sabrina! I need a Bud Light in a bottle - yesterday!" Reuben nodded in agreement.

"I guess you two will do," Sabrina said and sighed.

With puzzled looks, the two off-duty policemen huddled with their favorite bartender.

***

When police cars come screaming up to a place like The Boiler Room, it doesn't take long for the crowd to clear out. Several squad cars were parked at odd angles out front, lights flashing, sirens now silenced. A flock of officers milled about, smoking and talking in hushed tones, "protecting" the crime scene. Another contingent stood guard by the alley, where the coroner's hearse was parked. In small Mississippi towns like Indian Springs, an unexplained death was big news, and policemen from far and wide, deputy sheriffs as well as state troopers, raced to the scene to offer "assistance." A potential murder was like a soap opera made for men, and it was a juicy one for the boys who wore the badge.

One officer confronted Joshua at the bar, while another one questioned Sabrina in the billiard area. Darnell Dupont, the only detective in Indian Springs, gave Joshua his most intimidating glare and sized him up quickly. He noted that Joshua was tall and lean, but he also saw that he was strong - Army strong. He also noted a hint of sadness about his eyes, just as Sabrina did. Joshua had the look of a man who had seen some things out there in the world, some of them bad, very bad.

Dupont, fit and trim himself, sharp in black suit and tie, asked, "So, who are you?"

"Joshua. Joshua MacMillan."

"I don't know any MacMillan's around here. You must be new in town. Where you from?"

"Asheville. North Carolina," he added to clarify.

"How did you get all the way down here?" As Joshua explained, the detective eyed him sharply, thinking that there was more to the story. "Where you staying?" he asked.

"Little embarrassed to say, but I'm staying upstairs in the old theater, with permission, though, until I can find a place. In the meantime, the fellow down at the garage is looking for a used engine for me. At least this is walking distance, for now," Joshua said and chuckled nervously.

The detective did not chuckle in return. Or crack a smile. "Let's get down to the nitty gritty. How do you know Dee Dee Scarborough?"

"I mean, she comes into the bar a lot, but that's it."

"You sure about that?"

"Like I said, I'm new in town."

"And you were taking out the trash when you found the body?" Joshua nodded yes. "Can somebody vouch for your movements tonight?"

"Wait, do you think...?" Dupont stared impatiently at him, his eyes demanding an answer. "Sure. I've been here since four. Left just the once to take out the trash. Sabrina can tell you."

"And when you found the body, you came right back in? Didn't touch anything?" Again, Joshua nodded yes. "What about

Sabrina? Was she in the bar all night, as well?

"Yeah, I think so. I don't think she left. We were pretty busy tonight."

"Well, can I find you here if I need to ask you anything else?"

"Sure. I'm not going anywhere. Getting my bus fixed might take a minute."

Dupont gave him his hard police stare again, before striding away purposely to join the other officer interviewing Sabrina. As he turned away, the door from the theater dressing room burst open, banging against the doorpost, and Scott strode in, clearly alarmed.

"Sabrina! What the hell is going on?"

"It's Dee Dee. She's dead," Sabrina said shakily. Scott's eyes widened, and a look passed between them, a look that Joshua caught. Detective Dupont didn't miss it, either.

Then, the detective said to Scott, "I'm going to need to talk to you next." Joshua could see Scott swallow hard. "After we get done talking, I'm gonna' need ya'll to make a list of everyone who was in the bar tonight. What time did you last see Dee Dee?" he asked, addressing Sabrina.

***

Dee Dee's story made the news in nearby Jackson, but she also made the news as far away as Memphis and New Orleans. Her funeral was like a made-for-TV docudrama, and the tearful images of her little daughter Haley and the somber expression of her husband Paul were iconic, burned into Mississippian's memory. People talked about it at the grocery store, and they gossiped about it in church parking lots.

The next Wednesday night, Joshua was on duty at The Boiler Room, but Sabrina was off. It was church night in town and the pub was usually slow, but since Dee Dee Scarborough was found dead in the bar's alley, business at The Boiler Room had picked up. Her death was the talk of the town, and everyone wanted to know what the bartender heard. After all, bartenders hear everything, but they know better than to tell anything.

Except to other bartenders.

With the night being busier than usual, Sabrina dropped in to check on things. "Has it been this steady all night?" she asked. Joshua nodded yes, then caught her up on the beer and liquor deliveries, assuring her that they had plenty for the weekend. Somebody put a quarter in the jukebox, and Van Halen's "Jump" blasted from its speakers.

"So," Joshua began, speaking a little louder over the music, "Have you heard anything else about Dee Dee and you know...?"

Sabrina's face darkened, and she was slow to reply. "Not really, but the word on the street is that they have recovered the bullets and ID'd the caliber."

"Was that word from one of your off-duty friends?"

"Could be."

"You know, I wonder what she was doing out there anyway."

"Well, whenever Dee Dee came to the bar she always parked in the alley where employees park." Joshua looked puzzled. Seeing the look, Sabrina said, "You saw her white BMW convertible out there, right? Pretty recognizable. The only one like it in town. I think she parked out there to avoid curious eyes, especially her husband Paul's."

"What's her story anyway? You told me she was a flirt, which I could have figured out myself, but what's the rest of her story?"

"Well, what I heard is that she grew up hard, got married young, shotgun wedding and all. Then, the guy split and left her with a little girl. She got a job at the casino on the Choctaw Indian Reservation over near Philadelphia, Mississippi. She was a dealer, I think. Blackjack."

"How did she wind up here in Indian Springs?"

"That's where her husband Paul comes in. Seems he likes to gamble, and he liked the younger ladies after his divorce, or maybe before, who knows? Dee Dee was young and cute, he was well-to-do, and he looked like a potentially good daddy for little Haley. So, the rest is history."

"Still, I don't understand. Detective Dupont, he seemed like he suspected me, you, Scott, all of us. Why?"

"A lot of people couldn't stand Dee Dee, including me, so I guess he has to question everybody."

He continued to wipe down the bar silently, before another thought occurred to him. "You said something the other night that got me curious." Another quarter, and the jukebox began playing the Rolling Stones' "Honky Tonk Women." With an amused glance at the record machine, he asked, "You said that it was hard to tell sometimes that she was married. What did you mean? Was she more than a flirt?"

"Well," Sabrina began slowly, "Dee Dee had a reputation. She enjoyed being in the plays, in the community theater, as you know." Her face darkened again. "The rumor is that she 'liked' the younger actors, if you know what I mean. Oldest story in the book. Younger wife, older husband, temptation...."

Joshua wondered if Scott was one of those younger guys. He remembered the looks that passed between Sabrina and Scott whenever the subject of Dee Dee arose.

"Well, whatever happened, I guess she got what she deserved. Like they say, 'what goes around, comes around,'" Sabrina said.

After a pause, Joshua said, "That's usually true, but not always. Sometimes bad things happen to good people, too."

The look on his face told Sabrina that he had been there, done that.

KERRY MACK WRIGHT

CHAPTER FOUR
"Cheeseburger in Paradise"

It was late when Joshua got his work done at the bar. The Boiler Room closed on "Thirsty Thursdays" at 11, but by the time he cleaned the bathrooms, restocked the coolers, swept the floor, and took out the trash, it was well past midnight. He felt restless, so he set out walking across the town square past the library, dodging the giant Magnolias. The night was hot and still, and cicadas droned in a mindless, annoying symphony. He was beginning to wonder if he was stuck in Indian Springs. Not that there was much of anything left for him in North Carolina, but he questioned his decision to stay and rescue his VW. And yet, where else should he be?

He also felt hungry. He had heard about a little "greasy spoon" that was in an old gas station, of all places. Not sure if it even had a name, but for some reason, it stayed open most all night, so they said. He was told that they made the best cheeseburgers in the world, a genuine "Cheeseburger in Paradise," as the Buffet song went. Supposedly, they used fresh-ground, never-frozen beef, and they patted out their burgers by hand. And their beer was ice cold. Sounded like a good night to find out, he thought.

A single light was burning in the store front, and a bell jingled as he went inside. Didn't seem like anyone was home. There was a single table in the dimly lit room, and there was one pool table towards the back. A man wearing a grease-stained white apron, looking remarkably like an older Stanley Kowalski, came out from the back. He gave Joshua a suspicious scowl.

After a moment of stony silence, he finally growled, "What'll ya' have?"

"I want one of your famous cheeseburgers," Joshua said

and smiled.

"Good, 'cause that's all we serve! And don't tell me how you want it. I fix 'em one way - my way." With that, he turned and shuffled back into the other room.

A minute later, a disembodied, raspy female voice proclaimed," If you need something to drink with your burger, hun, just reach in the cooler around the corner and grab what you want." Her voice sounded like whiskey and cigarettes.

Startled, Joshua reflexively replied, "Yes, ma'am!"

In the small chest cooler, he found only Budweiser in the can. That was it, nothing else. Popping the top on a cold one, his eyes wandered around the room. There were faded, tin prints of dinosaurs on the dingy walls. Taking a long, cold slurp of his brew, he realized the significance. This used to be a Sinclair service station back in the day, and the dinosaur was their symbol. He could still catch a whiff of grease, used motor oil, and kerosene.

"Why don't you take a load off?" the voice invited.

Looking up, Joshua saw an older white woman, her short, graying hair in curls. She smiled, showing her cigarette-stained teeth, as she wiped her hands on an old-fashioned, flower-print apron. With a loud screech, he scraped a chair out from under the table. Circa 1950's, the table had a red Formica top with silver, metal legs; the chairs were mismatched but comfortable with plush stuffing, some of which was coming out of their splitting, red vinyl covers.

As he sat down, she rasped, "What's your name, sugar?"

"Joshua. What's your name?"

"Well, now, before we git too personal, I want to know a little more about you." She spat her words out like miniature coughs. "But I do like your name. A good Bible name."

"Well, I'm new in town."

"That's obvious."

"I work at The Boiler Room."

"Tell me something I don't know."

"I'm working so I can get my broken-down VW fixed.

Needs a new engine."

"That's what Joe at the garage told me," she grinned, as she lit a Chesterfield. "What's the rest of your story?"

"That's what I'd like to know," Detective Dupont said, as he emerged from the kitchen with two plates, each filled with a giant cheeseburger and a mountain of home-cut French fries.

"I didn't know you worked as a server on the side," Joshua quipped, noting that Dupont was out of uniform.

Plopping the two plates on the table, the officer said, "You never know where I might turn up."

Joshua's stomach growled as he eyed his loaded burger. The patty must have weighed half-a-pound before it was cooked. One bite later, and he was moaning and licking his lips.

"I only thought I'd had a good burger before. This is perfect," he said, sighing and wiping a line of juice from his chin.

"Good!" the woman said. "I'll tell Frankie to put his pistol back in his holster."

Joshua's eyes widened, but Dupont chuckled before taking a bite of his burger. Dipping a fry in some ketchup, he winked at the woman, and she disappeared into the back.

Looking Joshua dead in the eye, chewing his fry, he said, "So, yeah. I would like to know the rest of the story. I'm not asking politely like Auntie Flo; I'm asking like a police detective."

He wondered what the detective would ask and how much he should tell.

"Fair enough," he said. "I'm a stranger. Questions shouldn't come as a surprise in a small town like this."

"Were you Army?" Dupont asked, ignoring his comment.

"Yeah. How did you know?"

"Got the look about you."

"If you recognize 'the look' as you say, you must have served, also."

"Yes, I did, but you first."

"OK. Knew I was gonna' get drafted right out of high school - no money for college. The Army recruiter told me that if I enlisted, things could go better for me. I was thinking that at least the Army would get me out of that single-wide on the hill, and it did - straight from the hills of North Carolina to the hills of Vietnam."

"Who'd you serve with?"

"The 525th MI Group."

"Military Intelligence?" Dupont raised an eyebrow.

"Yes. Trained at Ft. Bragg, North Carolina for two years and was stationed at the Tan Son Nhut Air Base in Saigon."

"How did you get assigned to intelligence?"

"Turns out I had a knack for language, so they taught me French and Vietnamese."

"So, you were one of them REMF's, who didn't see any action!"

Joshua hadn't heard that expression in a long time. "Rear Eschelon Mother...."

"Well, that's what you would have thought. I was hoping that I had got lucky, but as it turns out, they didn't always have enough interpreters. Often, they would 'volun-tell' me to fly by chopper to some God-forsaken place in the boonies to help gather intel from the locals. Half the time, I didn't know which side of the Cambodian border I was on." A troubled, brooding look took over Joshua's face, and he stopped talking.

"So, you saw some bad stuff, hunh?"

As if jarred from a reverie, Joshua said, "I saw some stuff that didn't get on the news, some stuff you won't ever read about in history books. I really don't want to talk about this anymore."

"OK. What about when you got back to the world?"

"Well, I thought I would serve only a one-year tour in 'Nam, like everyone else, but they told me at the last minute that I would have to stay another year. They said I was technically a non-combatant, and they had spent so much money training me. I was screwed, but the good news was that when they sent me back to Ft. Bragg in '72 I had finished my active service. The first year I was in the Reserves, I tended bar for a friend. Then in '73 I went to Appalachian State on the GI Bill. My goal was to become a history teacher, so I could help students understand what happened in 'Nam. That way, maybe we wouldn't repeat our mistakes. I wound up being a History Major and French minor and got a job teaching high school American history and Intro French."

"Well, laissez le bon temps rouler!" Dupont said, grinning.

"I was thinking your name is French."

"Well, I guess you are going back to teach at the end of the summer?"

Joshua paused and frowned. "I don't really know. I was kinda' at a place where I wasn't sure if I wanted to keep teaching, anyway, and now, I'm kinda' stuck here." The frown was replaced with a wistful look.

The detective thought that he still didn't have all his story.

"So, what about you?" Joshua changed the subject.

"Got drafted. Did a one-year tour in country, and then they sent me to Germany. I thought, 'I made it out alive, and I'm going to Europe!' Way better than picking Jim Crow cotton down in Mississippi. But it was crazy. We were supposed to be protecting the Germans from a Russian invasion, but a lot of the folks didn't want us there, especially black guys like me. There was racial trouble, in the service and out, and some vets from 'Nam were committing suicide. On top of that, too many soldiers were drunk-driving their way into telephone poles. That's how I became an MP. Huge need at the time, so I stayed in the Service a while. Got to travel around Europe. Paris was great! The ladies there loved fellows like me," he said and laughed.

"How did you wind up back here in Mississippi?"

"Eventually, got tired of the crap and came home. Like you, I used the GI Bill to go to school - Jackson State - and majored in Criminal Justice. Got a job in Indian Springs, my hometown of all places, so here I am."

"By the way, how did you know I was here for a burger tonight, anyway?"

"Connections," he said with a wink.

"Do you have any suspects? Besides the usual ones?"

Joshua grinned at his *Casablanca* reference.

"If I did, I couldn't tell you," the officer said, no nonsense.

"What can you tell me?"

"You sure you're not still in intelligence? You ask a lot of questions."

It was Joshua's turn to smile. "Well?"

"As for other suspects, there were a lot of people at the bar that night. It might have been one of them, or maybe not. When someone dies, you always look for motive and opportunity. With murder the motive is usually money, revenge, or rage. Opportunity? Who was close enough to do the deed? With a woman like Dee Dee, there are always possibilities. You had opportunity, but I don't see a motive. Not yet, anyway."

Feeling another presence in the room, Joshua and Dupont looked up to see Miss Flo and Mr. Frankie staring at them.

"Ya'll can go now that you're done. We're gonna' close up," Frankie growled. Flo coughed and gagged in agreement.

"All right. Good night Auntie Flo and Uncle Frankie. See you later." He said "auntie" like "awn-tea." With a puzzled look, Joshua's mouth opened as if to ask a question. Before he could, the Detective spoke. "That's a story for another cheeseburger," he said with a laugh. "We need to let them close up."

"Wait!" Auntie Flo commanded. Both men stopped and looked at her expectantly. "If you want, Joshua, we got a room to rent. Not much, but don't cost much, neither." The detective looked at her in surprise.

"That would be great!"

"Come by tomorrow and we'll work it out. I've got a good feeling about you," she said warmly.

He wondered if a friendship was brewing, in more ways than one. That was fine by him.

***

The apartment was going to work out fine. He settled up with "Awn-tea" Flo earlier, so tonight, he would take his things over after work. The apartment was small and simple, but it came with a couch and a bed, which was a good start. It was in a house halfway up the hill on Washington Avenue, which was still within walking distance of the bar. The large white house was a mishmash of apartments. Flo and Frankie owned the old home, lived in one of the apartments, and rented out the rest.

His apartment had a kitchen and living room in a sub-basement, which could be accessed from the gravel parking lot in the back of the building. He would park his VW there, if he ever got it back. From there, it was down three steps to a small patio and then into the kitchen. To the right was the living area, which contained a gas space heater in a faux fireplace. There were built in bookshelves on either side. On the left and up three steps was a doorway to the first-floor hallway. That hallway led to other apartments, a set of stairs to the second floor, and to a large front porch that overlooked the other houses on the descending street. From his living area, he could ascend some narrow stairs on the right to his bedroom and bathroom on the second floor. Interestingly enough, his bedroom door opened to a second-floor hallway where there were more apartments. All in all, not bad. He had a real place to sleep, eat, and clean up. No more cold showers in the moldy locker room.

One problem solved, at least, but not before another one began a few days later. As Joshua walked down the street to the bar, he could see the TV news trucks parked outside. He noted stations from Jackson, Greenwood, and Memphis. Right now, they were beaming shots of reporters in front of The Boiler Room to their home stations via satellite. Curious bystanders were watching and listening.

Before anyone could spot him, he dodged left into the alley, the same alley where Dee Dee died, so he could enter through the side door. Safe for now. As he checked the beer cooler under the bar, he remembered what Detective Dupont had said. When it comes to murder, you must ask who had motive and who had opportunity. Motive: if Dee Dee were cheating on her husband, Paul Scarborough was an obvious suspect. But he was nowhere around when she died at the bar. Well, no one saw him at any rate. Of course, he could have hired someone to do it,

Joshua mused. Or does that stuff only happen in the movies?

His tasks completed, it was time to open. He unlocked the front door and flipped the sign hanging on it to "Open." As he did so, he continued to think about the crime. What about Scott Goodman, the theater director? Joshua saw the look in his and Sabrina's eyes. Was Scott cheating on her? Was Sabrina about to find out about an affair? Did Dee Dee plan to leverage their secret into a more permanent relationship with Scott? What about opportunity? Well, apparently, he was right next door in the theater at the time she died.

And then, there was Sabrina. If Scott were cheating, jealously and rage, plain and simple, would have been her motive. Joshua had seen how angry Sabrina had gotten over Dee Dee's flirting and dancing with Scott. And serving drinks at the bar would have been an opportunity to slip out back and do the deed. Like the detective said, even Joshua had that opportunity, just no motive. Still, Sabrina and Scott were very good to him. Hard to imagine either one of them as a killer. That was when Joshua remembered with a start that Sabrina had been missing for a while that night. Even good people can lose their cool and do something stupid, he mused.

The door opened, and a lovely young woman dressed in a business suit sauntered in. Great! thought Joshua. A reporter!

"Why, hello there!" she called out flirtatiously.

Seriously?

"What would you like?"

"What I would like is some information. I'll take a Bud Lite." She sat at the bar and looked at him like a hungry orca eyeing a baby seal. She was clearly reading him, looking for an angle to get him to talk.

"OK, out with it. What's on your mind?" he asked.

"My name is Shannon Newcombe, and I'm with Channel Six in Greenwood. I'm surprised you didn't recognize me."

"I don't watch much television, especially the news."

"Anyway," she continued, "what's it like to have someone murdered outside your place of business?"

"What do you think?"

"I heard you were the one who discovered the body. What was that like?"

Fortunately, folks were beginning to filter in, so he excused himself to fill other drink orders. She was relentless, however.

"What did she look like when you found her?"

"I really don't want to talk about this, OK?"

"I understand, but our viewers want to know what happened. They need to know...."

"Do they really?" Joshua interrupted churlishly, staring her down.

Undeterred, she smirked and said, "Any thoughts on who killed her?"

The jukebox screamed into action with Michael Jackson's "Beat It." Joshua grinned, hoping the reporter would get the message. "Just beat it, beat it, beat it...." In the meantime, he was intent on keeping his mouth closed. Sensing that she was getting nowhere with him, the reporter finished her beer and slipped her card on the table.

"If you think of anything, anything at all, don't hesitate to call me," she said, smiling and batting her eyes suggestively as she turned and left the bar.

He huffed and muttered, "Good grief!"

CHAPTER FIVE
"The Usual Suspects"

Tuesday night was slow. Too slow. The sizzle of gossip about Dee Dee had simmered down. Then, the theater dressing room door opened, and Scott Goodman walked in. He plopped down on a barstool and asked for a Coors Lite. Joshua reached into the cooler, retrieved the cold beer, popped the top, and put it down on a bar coaster in one smooth movement. After taking a long pull on his beer, Scott said, "The shows won't be the same now that Dee Dee is gone."

Joshua's interest was piqued, so he asked, "Why is that?"

"You saw her in *Streetcar*. She was the best actor we had. She was very versatile, too."

"Sounds like you miss her."

"Oh yeah, definitely. She will be missed," he said, as he took another long pull of his beer. Joshua wondered what that meant in Scott's case. "I know people didn't have a high opinion of her, I know all of that, but she was actually good people."

Why is he defending her? Joshua wondered.

"I mean, I know people thought she was loose and stuff, but that's not the person I knew."

"Really? That's not what I heard."

"Well, don't get me wrong, she liked to flirt and all, but deep down inside, she was very loyal to her friends, and to her husband."

"Really," Joshua couldn't help but repeat.

"Yeah, she told me all about her childhood, growing up tough and all, getting pregnant and getting married so young. Her husband cheated on her and then ditched her. She vowed she would never cheat like that, because she knew how it felt to be on the losing end. Paul was really good to her and Haley, and I think, despite her reputation, she would never have done anything to hurt him."

"Then why was she such a flirt?"

"I don't know. Maybe she learned to do it working at the casino. You know, better tips. Maybe the attention she got from flirting - and acting – made her feel better about herself. On the other hand, being so much younger than Paul, maybe she still wanted to dance and party, but just not party in that way. Who knows?"

"Man, that's not what people say."

"Tell me about it!" Scott said, making Joshua wonder about Mark and Sabrina's conversations on the subject.

"Tell me something, man-to-man. Were you ever tempted by her flirting, you know, working late with her on her lines?"

Scott gave Joshua a long "none of your business" look before answering.

"I should probably tell you, 'Nah, never!' But what the heck, let's be honest. Dee Dee was hot, so yeah, any guy would think about it, but Sabrina has been with me through my ups and downs. And you get a lot of those in my line of work. I would never do that to her. I love her, man. And I don't think Dee Dee would ever take it that far, anyway." With that, he finished his beer thoughtfully, gently placed it on the bar, and said, "Gotta' go, man. Time to work on what we're gonna' do for the next show."

"Break a leg!"

"We'll do our best. See ya' later, man," he said as he headed to the dressing room door in the back.

Scott seemed convincing. It didn't sound like he had anything going on with Dee Dee, but you never know. If he did, he would lie, right? What Joshua wondered was if Scott was able to convince Sabrina. And for that matter, did Paul believe these things? And, did Detective Dupont know this side of the story?

**

It was late on Saturday night, actually early on Sunday morning, when Joshua and Sabrina finished shutting down the bar. Since they were not open on Sundays, and Monday was slow, Joshua had a couple of days off. They bid farewell, Sabrina presumably headed home to Scott, and he to his new place. As he walked toward his apartment, he realized that he was craving another cheeseburger. Detouring from his usual route home, he headed towards the back street where the old gas station with its amazing burgers was located.

Once again as he entered, the bell tinkled, but the place seemed deserted. He plopped down at the dilapidated table to wait. No one came. It was very quiet, too quiet. Joshua hoped nothing was wrong with Miss Flo or Mr. Frankie. He flinched when a voice sounding like someone gargling gravel shouted, "Be there with you in a minute, hon!"

"What a voice!" Joshua muttered.

"You want the usual, sugar?" Miss Flo asked, appearing suddenly from the back, wearing the same stained, flower-print apron. Joshua nodded, and she said, "Well, you know where the beer is!"

Joshua crossed over to the cooler, plucked out a beer and popped the top. "Man, this stuff is so cold. Just what I needed after a long night on my feet." He turned to Miss Flo, but she was already gone.

Reappearing from the back, Miss Flo asked, "How are things working out with the apartment?"

"It's great!"

"Do you have everything you need? If not, the best place to go is to the Gibson Discount Center out on the main highway. Their prices are the best."

"That's a good tip, thanks, but that's quite a walk."

"Just let me know, and Frankie will give you a ride."

"Thanks, that would be great."

"How's it coming at Joe's garage?" she asked, a sly grin on her face.

"No luck."

"Hmmm. That's unusual. Joe is always able to find what he needs."

What's up with that grin? Joshua wondered. And then, there he was again. Detective Dupont walked out from the back, a plate in each hand, each one piled high with a burger and fries.

"Your day job must not pay very well, detective."

"Call me Darnell. That's easier to say than Detective Dupont."

"OK, sure. Does that mean we are going to be friends?"

"Hmmm. We'll see."

And then they dove into their meal, like condemned men eating their last supper at Parchman Farm, the state penitentiary. With contented sighs, they pushed back their plates and polished off their beers.

"Hey, Detective, I mean, Darnell, I might have a tip for you. You know, bartenders hear a lot of stuff, and we get paid to listen."

"Yeah, so?"

"I guess you know that Dee Dee was in the theater group, right?" Dupont nodded yes.

"I know you've heard the stories, so I figured that's why you wanted to talk to Scott and Sabrina. Had a conversation with Scott the other night at the bar. He has me doubting whether he had anything to do with Dee Dee, or her death, for that matter."

"Really. What did he say?"

"He said that Dee Dee was actually misunderstood. She was loose in reputation only. She just liked to flirt and party, but she was very faithful to Paul. Don't know if that helps in your investigation, but there it is." The detective huffed. Joshua continued, "I don't know, but my Army training taught me to read people pretty quickly. It was life or death in 'Nam, as you know. So yeah, I think he might be telling the truth."

"Maybe so, maybe so. But sometimes the truth doesn't matter as much as what people think is the truth."

"Do you have other suspects?" he asked, wondering if the detective was thinking of Sabrina and Dee Dee's husband Paul.

"You know I can't talk about that. Why are you so interested, anyway?"

The question caught Joshua off guard. He knew why he hated unsolved mysteries, especially life and death ones, but he was not ready to talk about that. He worried, too, that his interest might be misunderstood.

"I guess it was because I was there," he foundered.

Joshua wondered if the detective was beginning to focus on Sabrina. If he thought Scott was cheating with Dee Dee, did the detective think Sabrina would be the kind of person to do the deed? However, she seemed like a good person to Joshua, and she had been good to him. He just didn't think she had it in her. But still, everyone has a breaking point. That was something else he learned in 'Nam.

"You got quiet all of a sudden."

"Sorry, just wondering about something. I heard ya'll have the bullets and identified their caliber," Joshua said.

"Now, where did you hear that?"

"Bartender, remember? So, did you?"

"Maybe."

"And?"

"And what?"

"What caliber were they?"

"OK. Cards on the table. I don't know how far I can trust you yet, but Aunty Flo thinks highly of you. Not sure why. But she is a good judge of character, so I have learned to trust her judgement. I guess it won't hurt to tell you, if you can keep your mouth shut. They were .22's."

"Hmmm. The killer used a 'Saturday Night Special.'"

"Right. The favored weapon of rookies and professionals alike. Small, lightweight, easy to conceal. Not as noisy as a .38 or a .45, but any doctor will tell you they can do a lot of damage, especially up close. And easy to dispose of, too."

"So, if you could find that gun and match the bullet, that would be a big step forward. But who and how?"

"What do you think?" the detective asked.

"Well, her husband Paul Scarborough would have motive, if he thought Dee Dee was messing around," Joshua noted.

"What did he say when you interviewed him?"

The detective gave no answer.

"Look," Joshua said, exhaling in exasperation. "I have some interest in this case, and I have learned some skills in intelligence. That doesn't make me a cop, but as a bartender, I could make a pretty good source."

"Maybe. I don't know."

"I can tell you don't think I was involved in the murder. So, at some point you are either going to trust me or not; we are going to be friends or not."

"Fine. I can tell you that we haven't interviewed him," Darnell said, looking up at the ceiling with a pained expression.

"Why?"

"The Chief said to hold off."

Joshua was stunned.

"Maybe it has something to do with the fact that Mr. Scarborough is the biggest employer in the town. In fact, this town would sink without that refinery, without the money it pumps into the economy. The Mayor is leaning on the Chief to give it time, to let it play out on its own. 'Give the man a chance to grieve,' he said."

"Oh, man!"

"Yeah, well, it stinks. When a woman is murdered, the first suspect, the usual suspect, is the husband. And this trail is getting colder by the hour."

"So, what are you going to do?"

"Look for that pistol. In the meantime, I suppose you could keep your ears open for me, barkeep."

"Roger that. Wait, doesn't she have an ex-husband somewhere?"

"Did not know that. That's good intel. I will have to check into that."

"Good. I'm headed out. See you later, Triple-D," Joshua said as he stood.

"Triple-D?" the detective lifted his eyebrows questioningly.

"Short for Detective Darnell Dupont."

"Triple-D. Not bad," the detective said, laughing and waving farewell.

CHAPTER SIX
"Something in the Way She Moves"

Joshua didn't mind walking to work; it was downhill on Washington, then a right on Jefferson, and a slight downhill grade all the way to The Boiler Room. The streets were tree-lined, and the smell of freshly mowed grass was in the air. It was Friday, it was hot, and it was going to get hotter tonight, since they had a special guest playing. Son Thomas, a local legend, could really wail when he played slide guitar and sang the blues.

Suddenly, Joshua stopped short. Looking down the street towards the bar, he saw police cars everywhere. He started to jog, his stomach growing queasy. When he reached The Boiler Room, he saw Sabrina out front. Her arms were crossed as she paced back and forth on the sidewalk, tears leaking from her eyes.

"Sabrina!" he called out. "What's happening?"

"Joshua! I'm glad you're here." She choked back a sob. "I had just come in and was beginning the bar prep when the door burst open, and there were police everywhere. They served me with a search warrant, and they are tearing through the place!"

"Oh, Sabrina, I am so sorry!"

On top of that, Detective Dupont just turned me out after grilling me about Dee Dee's death. And he... he asked me if I knew anything about it! They suspect me!"

"Oh.... really?" Joshua said, suddenly feeling very guilty, wondering if he had somehow helped lead the detective's mind in Sabrina's direction.

"He said that I was angry with her because I thought she was having an affair with Scott!"

"Did you think that?"

"Yes! And Scott and I had several fights about it."

"What did Scott say?"

"He denied it, of course!"

"Do you believe him?"

"I don't know what to believe! All I know is they think I wanted revenge, so I killed her!"

Sabrina began to cry, and he put his arm around her shoulder. Scott walked up to the two of them, having heard their last few remarks. He and Sabrina embraced, Sabrina sniffling, anguish in Scott's face.

"I've been trying to tell you, sweetheart. There was nothing to it! I love you! I would never cheat on you!" Scott promised. "And I know that you would never hurt anyone, much less kill someone."

The local PD began to file out of the bar, followed by Detective Dupont, who was the last to leave. Scott and Sabrina both gave him a stony look, while Joshua looked at him questioningly. He returned their looks with a solemn face that masked all emotion. However, an evidence bag was swinging from his hand as he walked. The shape of a pistol could be seen in it.

The detective approached Sabrina. "You are going to need to come down to the station with us," he said to her. "I have some more questions for you."

"Why?"

"Need to ask you about the .22 pistol we found stashed in the broom closet."

"I promise ya'll I don't know anything about Dee Dee's murder," Sabrina exclaimed.

"I believe you!" her husband assured her, as the detective led her to his squad car.

The last Joshua saw her, tears were sliding down Sabrina's face as she looked back at them through the squad car window. He wondered if her tears were tears of regret or tears of guilt? Maybe the tears came from her fear. And then Scott was racing to his car to drive to the police station.

Joshua asked himself what he should do. Should he just go back to work, like nothing happened? He reasoned that the only thing he could do for Sabrina right then was to open the bar and keep it going. And let's hope that the bullets that killed Dee Dee don't match that pistol, he reasoned.

***

Son Thomas was amazing, and the crowd was crazy, so Joshua "stayed in the weeds" all night. He just couldn't catch up. At least the sales were good. He raced to fill drink orders and deliver food orders to the table.

And then, it happened. Everything seemed to slow down in his mind, like a football play shown in slow motion on TV. There she was! Right there! Dancing with the crowd. Something about the way she moved. The same glowing, brown skin. The same long black hair and dark eyes so big, a fellow could get lost in them. And then the world stopped, like a movie frozen on one frame, as he stared, mouth open. Was it really HER, or was he just seeing things? It couldn't be. He felt like he was seeing a ghost. And then, everything seemed to go back to regular speed, and she was gone, lost in the crowd of dancers. Joshua strained to see her again, but to no avail. He sighed, knowing he would not get much sleep tonight.

It was a long walk home to his apartment after he closed. Sleep took even longer, even as tired as he was, but when he finally slept, he dreamed of North Carolina and the lush Smoky Mountains. He dreamed of cascading waterfalls and creeks bubbling and murmuring over smooth stones. He dreamed of that night in Asheville with Adsila, his "blossom," as she opened to him, dancing together in the moonlight to the Beatles' "Something in the Way She Moves". His arm around her waist, her head on his chest, their bodies fitting seamlessly together. In fact, he couldn't tell where her body ended and his began. His right hand on the soft, smooth nape of her neck, his face buried in her hair, the smell so vivid. It was a fragrance that reminded him of sunshine and blue sky and fresh-cut mountain flowers.

"Where are you now, my Cherokee Rose?" he murmured in his sleep.

***

Tuesday came, and Mr. Joe said he "might" have found an engine for the VW. Holding on to hope, it was back to work for Joshua. Within minutes of opening, someone had punched Journey's "Don't Stop Believing" on the jukebox. He sighed. A few minutes later, Sabrina walked in.

"Sabrina! Good to see you!"

"Thanks. Good to be back."

"Well, you don't look any worse for the wear, as they say."

"It was no fun going downtown with Detective Dupont, believe you me. He kept pressing me about the .22 pistol they found here in the closet. I tried to tell him that it came with the bar. There always seems to be a raccoon or some other varmint tearing into the garbage, so the gun was to scare them off. And of course, I used it for that very purpose last week, which did not help my cause, since the pistol had obviously been fired recently."

"Did they take your fingerprints?" Sabrina nodded yes. "Did they take any from the gun?"

"Don't know for sure, but if they took my prints, they probably did."

"Well," Joshua posited, "They still would need to match the bullet to that pistol, and even if they do, that doesn't mean that you were the one who pulled the trigger."

"Unless there are no other prints on the gun but mine," Sabrina countered.

"Well, the bullet's not gonna' match!" he said encouragingly.

"Exactly, and that's what Scott and I kept telling the detective. In fact, I think that is the only reason they let me go. But what if the bullets do match? If they do, they will be back, and this time, they will have a warrant for my arrest."

"Haven't your off-duty friends showed up to support you?"

"Well, not officially, but in reality, I think they talked to Dupont. They know me, and they know I'm not a person who would kill someone."

"At least you have them on your side. Best case scenario, the bullets don't match the gun, and the police will have to move on to the next logical suspect."

"Who do you think that is?"

"Well, her husband Paul, for starters. Or her -ex."

"Absolutely!" Sabrina chimed in. "You saw how she danced with those men. If I had a wife who danced like that with a younger guy, I wouldn't put up with it."

The question is, did Paul put up with it? Joshua wondered.

***

Joshua could feel another cheeseburger run coming on; it was getting to be a habit. As he entered the old filling station, it was like Deja' Vu. First, the place was empty, then the disembodied voice took his order, and then Miss Flo appeared. And, like clockwork, Detective Darnell brought in plates of burgers and fries.

"We've got to quit meeting like this," Joshua deadpanned.

"Why?" asked Darnell with a sly grin.

"So, what's new?"

"What do you mean?"

"C'mon, man. You know what I mean."

"I do?"

"Do I have to spell it out for you? OK. You got the pistol from The Boiler Room, you took Sabrina's prints, and I'm guessing you dusted the pistol for prints. And?"

"And what?"

"You're just deliberately trying to tick me off, aren't you?"

"No," the detective replied. "Still wondering how much I can trust you. To keep your mouth shut, among other things."

"Remember what I said about bartenders? We keep our ears open, but we keep our mouths shut. So, whose prints were on the pistol?"

OK, OK. Sabrina's. And before you ask, no one else's."

"That's not good for Sabrina, especially if the bullets match that pistol," Joshua said. "When will you know?"

"We sent it to the lab in Jackson. It usually takes them a

couple of weeks to do the ballistics."

"I don't think the bullets will match."

"Why do you say that?" the detective asked.

"Would someone use a pistol to shoot somebody and then stash the gun where they work?"

"Unless they're not thinking straight. Believe me, in the heat of the moment, people have done stupider things than that."

"Yes, but after they settle down, they do start thinking straight. And that's when they throw the gun off the Choctaw River Bridge, where it'll never be seen again."

"You make a good point, but who says Sabrina didn't do it with another pistol, and she tossed that one? We just have to see this through. She had motive and opportunity. And whether you like it or not, so did Scott. Maybe. And the Mayor still won't let us talk to Paul Scarborough until we exhaust all other leads. In the meantime, if Paul is involved somehow, he's had plenty of time to cover his tracks."

"Have you had a chance to look into Dee Dee's ex-husband?"

"Yeah, we found out where he stays over near the Casino. We got some local PD to talk to him. Sounds like he has an iron clad alibi. He works second shift in a furniture factory, and his supervisor and co-workers vouched for him that he was at work that night. I guess that rules him out."

When they finished their food, Miss Flo bustled in to pull their plates. Her presence made Joshua remember something. "Hey, you remember I had a question about you and Miss Flo and Mr. Frankie? You said that was a question for a few more burgers. Well, we are way past that."

"OK, what do you want to know?"

"What exactly is your relationship with them? You call them aunt and uncle, but...."

"I get it. It's the early 80's, and while Jim Crow is technically dead, you and I both know that folks in the South generally stick to their own. Black folks and white folks have their own churches, their own clubs, and until about ten years ago, they had their own schools. Even so, the high school still hasn't had a prom since integration. They don't want the kids to mix."

"Unbelievable!"

"So, mixed marriages are still pretty rare. But hold on Mr. History Major, have I got a story for you! The Duponts were originally Catholics back in France, but some of them became Huguenots."

"French Protestants, gotcha'."

"Well, to escape persecution, some went to Canada, but some came to America. Over time, their descendants migrated down to N'Awlins. Some of the hardier ones came up the Mississippi River in search of land, and they found the Choctaw River. They negotiated their own treaties with the Choctaw natives, bought some land, and began to clear it for cotton. To begin with, they enslaved Indians to work the land. Later, they bought African slaves. A lot of folks don't know that the wealthiest Indians also bought African slaves. Anyway, the first thing you know, their fields grew into one big plantation, and that's where my explanation really starts."

"Go on."

"It was about 1835, when my namesake, my great-, great-grandfather, built himself a big mansion in the Delta down near the Choctaw River. He was all set to get himself a fancy wife, so he went down to N'Awlins to get one. He found a well-to-do, highly regarded British family, and he pretty much bought himself a wife. He made it worth her daddy's while, in other words. Her name was Agatha Scott Bentley, and he brought her to the Delta."

Darnell took a sip of his beer before he continued. "Well, she was used to life in civilized society, so to speak, and so after she gave him some children, she wanted to move to town to enjoy its social life. That big ole house you're living in? My namesake built it for her. It sits on the last hill before you git to the Delta, and they say Miss Agatha could see the plantation and its mansion from the widow's walk on top."

"Really? So, they lived apart?"

"Yes, and he was still a young man with a young's man's desires. He made many trips to N'Awlins, and he frequented the 'Octoroon Balls.'"

"I think I remember that from Southern History," Joshua said. "Octoroons were light-skinned people, and many of them could pass for white. However, they were considered black, even if they had only one-eighth African blood. Many of them were well-to-do and well-educated in New Orleans."

"Yes, and my ancestor found one to his liking. They entered into a relationship where, as his mistress, she had certain rights."

"I can't believe Agatha would put up with something like that!"

"Not only did she put up with it, but they say she liked that arrangement. Money and high society kept flowing through her home, and her children were healthy, wealthy, and wise."

"What about Mr. Dupont and his mistress? What was her name?"

"Evangeline."

"Beautiful name. Did they have children?"

"Yes, they had several children. So, what we have today are their descendants: the white Dupont's and the black Dupont's. Auntie Flo is a descendant of Dupont with Agatha, so the house in town was eventually handed down to her, and I am a descendant of him and Evangeline."

"So, who got the mansion in the Delta?"

"That would be General Sherman. He burned it down after the Battle of Vicksburg."

"And the land?"

"Agatha's people inherited it, but with the slaves being freed in the War, followed by Reconstruction, they began to fritter the land away. By the end of the Great Depression, nothing was left but the house on the hill."

"That is some story!" Joshua exclaimed. "What about

Evangeline?"

"Evangeline's children were given some land and property, but they eventually lost it. White folks made sure they couldn't make a living on it. They charged them too much for seed and supplies and paid too little for cotton. The County took it for back taxes."

"So, did the two sides of the family get along?"

"Most didn't…. Some barely did…. Even fewer really did."

"And you and Miss Flo and Mr. Frankie? I take it ya'll are in the 'really did' category?"

"They have been mighty good to me. Treated me better than a real aunt and uncle would."

"OK!" Auntie Flo interrupted. Time for ya'll to quit flapping your gums and go home!"

"Yes, ma'am," they replied together.

"See you next cheeseburger, boss," said Darnell. "Oh, one other thing you need to know." With a grin, he said, "Joe, at the garage? He's a Dupont, too. My cousin."

"Of course he is."

CHAPTER SEVEN
On the Lake

Mr. Joe found an engine. It was from a low-mileage vehicle that had been wrecked, and it was compatible with the van. Joe also had a lead on someone who could help him install it. The cost would be $600 because someone would have to pull the engine and then transport it to Indian Springs. He asked Joshua for half the money down and the other half when the work was done. Joshua agreed and paid him $300. Thank goodness his bartender gig included tips, and he was still getting his school check!

The summer was going by, though, and with his van fixed in a week or so, he could return to North Carolina. He just didn't know if he wanted to. He didn't really have a life there anymore, and he had made new friends in Indian Springs. He fit in well with the growing population of non-residents. And, he had a pretty good job here. He knew that if he were not returning to his teaching job, he would need to let his principal know soon. It was already pretty late to find a replacement. Still, there would be lots of history teachers looking for jobs, especially female teachers. Schools typically used history slots for men who could coach a sport. Thus, there was probably a woman out there who would be happy to take his job, so Joshua didn't feel too badly about it.

When he looked up, someone whom he had never seen before entered the bar. The man was wearing a charcoal gray suit with a starched white shirt and a yellow power tie, and his hair was stylishly cut and meticulously combed. He surveyed the room imperiously before spotting Joshua at the bar, after which he came over and took a seat. Joshua noted the age and worry lines on what would have otherwise been a handsome face.

"I want a shot of Tequila and a Lite beer in the can. I hear that's the drink of choice around here."

Interesting, he thought. As soon as Joshua served the drinks, the stranger slammed the Tequila and grimaced. Almost choking, he managed to swallow some of the beer to cool his throat.

"Good God!" he exclaimed. "How can anybody drink this crap?" More interesting, Joshua thought. The stranger continued. "I hear you are the one who found her."

"Excuse me?"

"Didn't you find Dee Dee out in the alley?"

And now it all made sense. This was Paul Scarborough, Dee Dee's husband.

"Yes," Joshua said.

A troubled look passed over Paul's face. He began as though he wanted to ask something. Instead, he chugged the rest of his beer and ordered, "Give me another round!"

Joshua was worried about where this would end up, but the customer is always right, so he served Paul his drinks. For his part, Paul looked askance at the Tequila, but still drank it, albeit one sip at a time, each followed by a sip of beer. It didn't take long for the buzz to hit.

"So, how well did you know Dee Dee?" he asked the bartender.

"I really didn't know her. I'm not from here, and I haven't been here long. Saw her in here a couple of times. That's all."

"I hear she used to really cut the rug in here with the boys." Joshua did not respond. Aided by the liquor, Paul's tongue began to loosen, and he said, "I loved that woman. I know she was a mess and a flirt, but I loved her. I think she loved me, too. And Haley. Lord! She misses her momma."

Like a good bartender, Joshua just listened. On the jukebox, "Yesterday" by the Beatles began to play, and Paul looked stricken. His shoulders sagged. Again, he struggled to ask a question. Sensing what it might be, Joshua started to answer, but his gut told him to wait. Paul sighed, and his eyes began to water. After a few more minutes of silence, he slid off the bar stool and slowly made his way out the door.

Now that's a crying shame, Joshua thought, and shadows of his own grief invaded his mind.

***

Joshua could tell that worry was beginning to take a toll on Sabrina. The lab reports were not back yet on the pistol, and she was wondering when the other shoe might drop. Furthermore, word was beginning to leak out that she was a suspect in the murder. Her friends on the police force had tried to keep such talk down, but people gossip, especially in small towns. Sabrina told Joshua that people began to stare at her in the bar. At least it had not made the local newspaper. Sensing the need to distract her, Scott set up a Sunday picnic outing with Greg and Shelly on their pontoon boat at a local lake. He invited Joshua to go, also.

"So, where is it we are going?" he asked.

"It doesn't really have a name. It's just one of the crescent lakes."

"Crescent lakes?"

"Yeah. The Choctaw River, like many rivers in the South, floods in the Spring. When it does, it erodes the banks in the bends of the river. Eventually, the banks collapse, and the river takes a new course. Over time, that part of the river is cut off by the new channel, and what are left are these lakes shaped like the crescents of the moon. They are narrow, like the river, and they are not very long."

"Now, that's an interesting geography lesson for a social studies guy," Joshua said with a grin.

The day was hot, but no one wanted to test the muddy water, since there could be snakes. Fortunately, the pontoon boat had a sunshade. It also had a large cooler full of sandwiches, snacks, and cold beer. Even dressed in cut-off shorts and t-shirts, the heat would have been brutal without the beer and the shade.

As they slowly puttered out to the middle of the lake, Shelly asked about the next play for the community theater. "So,

Scott, what do you think we will do for our fall show?"

"I don't know, but it needs to be a comedy."

Everyone shook their heads grimly in agreement, especially Sabrina.

"Any ideas?" Scott asked, as he turned on a portable radio. The static-filled sounds of "I Love Rock and Roll" by Joan Jett erupted from its tiny speakers.

"We have to think in terms of who we have and what types of roles they can play," Sabrina suggested.

"Well, comedy is different from drama," Scott responded. "Few actors can do both."

"I think Shelly can do both," Greg offered.

"Good!" Scott replied. "She could be a female lead."

"Maybe we should think about *Barefoot in the Park*," Sabrina suggested.

"That could work," Scott said. "Very small cast."

"You know who I think could be funny?" Joshua said. "Jeff and Reuben. The way they cut up at the bar. The way Reuben brought the house down when Jeff came on stage during Streetcar."

"Yeah, and Jeff handled a big role well for a rookie," Sabrina said.

"Maybe we should think about *The Odd Couple*," Shelly suggested.

Scott chuckled and said, "Oh, my goodness! Every police officer and his family within 50 miles would be there! Let me get some scripts, and we'll talk about it some more."

Suddenly, time seemed to slow down once again for Joshua. There she was, the same woman he had seen at the bar, the one who looked just like Adsila - his "Addie." Could it be her, or was he seeing things? This time, she was wearing cut-off blue jean shorts and a lime green halter top. She was sunbathing on a pontoon boat that was passing slowly by. As if in slow motion, she sat up and smiled and waved, her golden tan glistening in the sun. This can't be! Joshua thought. It just can't be. He was too stunned, too paralyzed to wave back. And then, she was gone.

Shaking himself as if from a dream, he stuttered, "Did ya'll see that?"

"See what?" Scott asked.

"That woman on the boat!"

They stared at him as if he were crazy.

"Of course we saw her! What's wrong with you?" Sabrina asked.

"You actually saw her. She was real?"

First Sabrina looked at Scott, and then he looked at Greg. Sabrina and Shelly looked at one another, puzzled, and then they all stared at Joshua.

"Uh, Joshua, are you OK?" Shelly asked.

"Maybe you've had too much sun and too many suds," Scott said and laughed.

"No, it's just that, I saw her before at the bar, and she looked just like somebody I know. Somebody I used to know, I mean. And that's probably not possible, so I thought maybe I was seeing things."

"Well, she was very real, and she was very beautiful," Scott said.

Sabrina gave him the stink eye and poked him in the ribs.

"Who is she?" Joshua asked.

"I don't know her name, but I've seen her out here before," Greg said. "Some guys from work and I go fishing down here sometimes, and we usually see her out here on a small bass boat with her dad. We just call her the 'Noodle Princess.'"

"What?! 'Noodle Princess?'" Joshua said, puzzled.

"Yeah, she looks like an Indian princess, and she's out here all the time 'noodling' for catfish."

"What's that?" asked Joshua.

"Well, I had never heard of it before I moved to Mississippi, but I couldn't believe my eyes the first time I saw her doing it."

"What did she do?" Shelly asked.

"Well, she and her dad locate a catfish hole, and they catch the fish bare-handed."

"No way!" Joshua exclaimed.

"I saw her do it. The local boys told me you stick your hand down in the hole and wiggle your fingers like floppy spaghetti. That's why it's called 'noodling.' Anyway, the catfish thinks it's live food and clamps down. When the fish clamps down on your hand, you shove it down its throat and grab it by the gills."

"Nunh-unh!" Joshua moaned.

"Yeah, I saw it. Then, she snatches it out of the water and throws it up on her shoulder. It was unreal! This beautiful young woman, smiling with this giant catfish on her shoulder. I just couldn't believe it the first time I saw it."

"'The 'Noodle Princess,' hunh? Well, at least she's real, even if your story is BS!" Joshua joked.

"I saw it!" Greg exclaimed.

"Alright, alright, I believe you! I'm just glad I wasn't seeing things."

"Have you ever tried it?" Scott asked.

"H-E-double hockey sticks, NO!" Greg exclaimed. "I'm not crazy!"

"I don't think it's crazy," Scott said.

"Yeah, coming from a guy who sucks crawfish heads back in Louisiana, you would say that," Sabrina said and laughed.

A few more beers later, and the day began to wane. Eventually, Scott said, "Time to pull back to the dock, I guess."

"Yeah, Sunday's about done, and Monday's coming," Greg agreed.

"But this was fun," Sabrina said. "I needed this. Thanks everybody."

Before long, the dock came into view, and so did a certain car parked beside it. The unmistakable profile of a police car stood out against the setting sun. And standing beside it was none other than Detective Darnell Dupont with his stony eyes. Sabrina inhaled sharply; all thoughts of a relaxing day gone. The detective looked like he had been waiting on them for a while. He also looked like a jury foreman ready to deliver a verdict to the judge.

    More likely, a police officer about to make an arrest.

CHAPTER EIGHT

August 1977

New Teacher Induction.

Hope that's nothing like military induction, Joshua thought.

What it was, was Monday through Friday, from eight to four, in mind-numbing "sit and get." Lectures on school procedures and discipline, professional ethics, lesson plan requirements, insurance, and retirement benefits. Forms, forms, and more forms to sign. He had a hard time concentrating, and not just because it was boring and his rear-end hurt. No, they had seated him next to a woman. And not just any woman. She was different. It wasn't just that she looked different in an amazing way; her very presence felt different. As they said in the 60's, she had a "vibe," and it was very natural - calm and appealing. No, not a vibe, an aura. She had an aura that made Joshua think of sunshine, fresh mountain air, and the smell of honeysuckles in the spring. Unlike him, she was focused on the task at hand, and she asked very intelligent questions.

Finally, on Wednesday, he couldn't take it anymore. Their only communication up to then had been a restrained, "Good morning" and "See you tomorrow." He wanted, he needed, to say something more to her. Summoning his courage, he finally spoke.

"Hey, by the way, my name is Joshua."

"I know," she replied. "I can read your name tag."

"Oh," he said and reddened. He hadn't even thought to look at her name tag. He couldn't stop looking at her big, dark eyes long enough to think about that.

Sensing his embarrassment, she hastened to say, "My name is Addie. Addie McCammon."

"Hey, Addie. Now I know why they put us next to each other. We are in alphabetical order. My last name is MacMillan."

This time she laughed. "Again, that is on your name tag, so I figured as much."

Joshua turned even redder, but he couldn't help himself - he couldn't shut up now that he had started. "I'm teaching American History at the high school. What about you?"

"American Literature, also at the high school."

"Oh! Is your curriculum organized thematically or chronologically?" Finally, he said something that he felt was semi-intelligent.

"Chronologically."

"Mine, too," he blurted out before he realized, of course it is; it's history, stupid! Why did he feel so awkward?

Ignoring his small blunder, she said, "Well, maybe we could build some projects together for our students, then," Addie said. "You know, you do the historical background, and I would do the related literature."

God, she is frigging brilliant, he thought. "That would be awesome!"

She smiled and her eyes crinkled delightfully. Before either of them could say more, the instructor began.

***

The next week was Pre-planning, which meant more boring meetings: faculty, department, and county-wide. There was little time left for making lesson plans and setting up his room. He wondered what his students would be like, and he both looked forward to meeting them and dreaded it. What if they don't like me? What if I don't like them? What if I'm not cut out to be a teacher? he worried.

Joshua rarely saw Addie since she was on the English Hall and he the Social Studies Hall. Once, in a faculty meeting, he thought he saw her glance his way, but that was it. So, when Friday finally came around, he decided to look her up and see how she was doing. Summoning his courage, he approached her room and saw an unexpected sign above her door. In Gothic lettering, it read, "Abandon all hope, ye who enter here."

Spotting Joshua staring at her sign, she walked out of her classroom and said, "Dante's *Divine Comedy*. Supposedly the sign over the entrance to hell."

"Oooo-Kay," he said. "Not very welcoming."

Grinning, she said, "Hey, I have high standards. I want to let my students know, tongue-in-cheek, that they had better buckle up."

"Let me know how that works out for you," he said doubtfully. "So, are you ready to meet the kids come Monday morning?"

"Yes, I'm very excited. Can't wait."

"Well, uh, I was kinda' wondering if you were still interested in doing some co-planning."

"Maybe, but for now, I need to stick to the basics until I get the students situated with my expectations and protocols."

"Oh!" he said, his disappointment evident. Pivoting, he said, "Good idea. But, ah, I was wondering if maybe we could get together after our first week with students and just think out loud for later. You know, in a broad strokes kind of way."

"What do you have in mind?" she asked, eyes twinkling.

"I hear they have really good cheeseburgers at this place called The Mountain Burger. Want to try them out? They only have a pick-up window, but they have picnic tables in the shade, so we could eat and talk there."

"OK, why not? You want to meet there at around 12?"

"Roger that!" Joshua exclaimed.

***

He arrived at The Mountain Burger early, to make sure things were as he was told. Sure enough, there were picnic tables, but better still there was a sizable line out front. That likely meant that the burgers were good. He found himself walking around a bit, pacing actually, as he waited for Addie to arrive. He worried that she might have forgotten, or worse still, that she would stand him up.

That was when Addie pedaled up on a vintage Huffy

bicycle. She wore her long, black hair in twin French braids, and the sun glinted off her Aviator sunglasses. Her white Bermuda shorts and lime-green tank top showed off her rich, brown skin. The physical workout of biking in the hills left her glowing, and she literally took Joshua's breath away.

"Hey, you made it!" he grinned.

"Did you doubt me?" she said smiling as she walked toward him, taking off her sunglasses.

"Uh, we better get in line," he stammered. He did not doubt her; he doubted if he was good enough for her.

Once they were served, they took their burgers, fries, and soft drinks to a shaded picnic table and sat. Joshua realized why the joint was called The Mountain Burger. It wasn't just because it was in the mountains of North Carolina; it was because the burgers were the size of mountains compared to other burgers. They dove in.

"That's a great cheeseburger!" he exclaimed.

"It is," Addie said, as she took the beef from her bun. She proceeded to eat hers like a lettuce and tomato sandwich, instead of a burger. Sensing Joshua was staring at her, she said, "What?" as she dipped a French fry in her ketchup.

"Uh, you're not eating the meat?"

"No, I'm sort of a vegetarian."

Then why did she agree to meet me at a burger joint, he wondered. After a pause, he understood and suppressed a grin.

"So, how was your first week?" he said.

"It was actually good. We got settled in, but the veteran teachers tell me the first two weeks is a honeymoon phase." Joshua wondered how her male students would be able to learn anything with someone as beautiful as her to distract them. "How about your first week?"

"A little bumpy at first, but it wound up being OK, I guess."

There was silence for a minute as they ate, then he said, "So, if we are going to be working together, we probably should get to know each other better. So, can I ask you a question?"

"May I?" she smiled.

"What?"

"It's may I, not can I."

"Oh." Joshua blushed.

"Just teasing. Sometimes I can't help myself. English teacher."

"May I ask you a question then?"

"Sure, if I may ask you one first," she said with a grin. "You seem a little older than a typical college graduate. How old are you?"

"You're right, I'm 26, going on 27."

"So, what were you doing before college? Working, or...."

"I was in the Army, in 'Nam, mostly."

"Ah, that explains it."

"Is that bad?" he asked.

"Of course not! Why would you say that?"

"It's just that a lot of folks called us some pretty bad things when we came home."

"Were you drafted? Some of my cousins were."

"I was about to be, so I joined up, to try to stay out of the worst of it."

"And were you able to do so?" she asked.

"Not always," he responded gloomily.

Sensing that it was a touchy subject, she said, "Now it's your turn to ask a question."

"OK, are you part Cherokee?"

"Yes, how did you know?"

"Well, being from North Carolina, I know several people with Cherokee blood. Your hair color and skin tone made me wonder. Please don't misunderstand; I think you're beautiful," he stammered. "Your skin, it's amazing. Nobody has a tan that good. It's like... like rich, caramel syrup, you know the kind you pour on ice cream on a hot summer day...." He stopped, mentally screaming at himself to shut up!

It was Addie's turn to blush. "Listen to you waxing poetic! Thank you." She tilted her head and grinned, as though observing him more deeply.

"And here's the other thing. Your hair, it's black, but in the sun, I can almost see some auburn tints."

"My mother was full-blooded Cherokee, a Youngdeer. Our family were tribal leaders at one point. My dad is Scottish all the way, a McCammon."

"Ah! That explains the auburn tints."

"My full name is Adsila Youngdeer McCammon. My Cherokee relatives call me Adsila, while my Scottish relatives call me Addie. When I started school, it was easier to tell the teacher I was Addie McCammon. Not that I am ashamed of my heritage or anything, but...."

"No need to explain. Kids can be cruel. Adsila is a beautiful name. What does it mean in Cherokee?"

"It means 'blossom.'"

"Ah! A Cherokee Rose!"

Once again Addie blushed, but she was quietly very pleased.

"Well, you must be Scottish, also," she said, using her fingers to comb his hair back from his eyes. "I see a hint of auburn in your hair, too."

The touch of her fingers tingled his scalp, and chill bumps dotted his arms. "Yes, mostly Scottish," he managed to say, "with a touch of Northern Ireland."

"What about your first name?" she asked. "It sounds kinda' biblical. Is there a story behind that?"

"Ha! I guess you could say that," he replied with a touch of annoyance. "My mom always told me that Joshua was a great man of God and a great leader, tall and strong. A conqueror. That's what she wished for me."

"So, she named you Joshua. A powerful name to help you begin your journey to the Promised Land, to your destiny."

"Never thought about it like that."

Anyone else might have laughed at his mother's beliefs, but Addie took another tack. She said, "I can see you are tall and strong, but are you a great leader?"

"Nah," he said grinning, her take on his name lightening

his mood. "Not yet, anyway," he said and laughed.

As they finished their food, the subject turned to potential projects, beginning with the Colonial period and its related literature.

Another week passed, and they again met for lunch on Saturday to decompress and talk about teaching. This time, Joshua insisted they go to Betty Lou's Diner, where they specialized in "meat and three" meals. They would have a veggie plate for Addie. Of course, the vegetables were flavored with pork, and he teased her about it.

"Nobody's perfect," she retorted, taking a forkful of black-eyed peas.

***

As September turned to October, he and Addie continued to see one another. The more they did so, the less they talked about school and lesson plans and the more they talked about themselves - their goals and their dreams. They talked about former boyfriends and girlfriends and realized that neither of them had been with anyone truly special. Lunches soon became dinners and then dinner and a movie. At their first movie, they saw *Raiders of the Lost Ark* and loved Harrison Ford in it, but the next time, the only thing playing was *Alien* with Sigourney Weaver. When the creature first appeared, hissing and drizzling its acid-filled saliva, Addie grabbed Joshua's hand and did not let go. In turn, he slipped his arm around her. He thought they fit just right.

A couple of weeks later, they went dancing at a nightclub in Asheville. They had a blast! Their first slow dance was to the Beatles song, "Something in the Way She Moves." That was when everything changed between them. In a good way. A very good way.

One Saturday in late October, when the leaves were at the peak of their fall color, the pair decided to hike to a secluded waterfall in the mountains. There, they would have a leisurely picnic midst the yellow, orange, and red foliage. It was a beautiful fall day, the sky a deep ozone blue with the temperature hovering in the 60's. A perfect day. Once they reached their destination, they spread a blanket next to the pool at the base of the waterfall. They shared a nice, but inexpensive red wine, fresh fruit, cheeses, crackers, and sandwiches. Their background music was the rushing water of the falls.

As they relaxed on their blanket, they began to talk. At one point in the wandering conversation, Addie asked, "So, tell me, what made you decide to be a teacher?"

"Hmmm. Good question," Joshua replied. "I think it was my experience in Viet Nam. So many good guys died, so young, so many hearts broken, and I'm not sure we accomplished much. When I got back to the 'world,' as we called it, I started reading up on the history of Southeast Asia to try to make sense of it. I didn't realize how much I enjoyed history, and so I decided to go to college to study it. As I did so, I began to understand its importance. As they say, 'Those who don't learn from history are doomed to repeat it.' I thought that maybe, in some small way, I could help young people learn from our tragic experience in 'Nam by teaching."

"Wow, that's very noble."

"How about you?" Joshua asked. "Why did you become a teacher?"

"That's easy. I love to read and write. I really enjoy poetry and trying to write it. So, becoming an English major and then a teacher was a no-brainer, as least for me."

"What kind of poetry is your favorite?'

"Oh, that's easy. Romantic poetry."

"You mean, like that gushy, love stuff?"

Addie laughed. "No, silly. Romantic poetry refers to poems written during the Romantic Age. You know, the age of individualism and rebellion and passion that was a reaction to the Age of Reason. The love of nature and the desire to return to it. They believed that people were born good, but a corrupt society corrupts us. Thus, they were generally against industrialization and the resulting displacement of people. They saw desperately poor children living in slums when they should have been living in Eden."

"Oh. I might have studied that in history. Sorry. Do you have a favorite Romantic poet?"

"For sure. That would be John Keats. His poetry was amazing, and some people thought he could have become another Shakespeare if he had not died so tragically."

"What happened?"

"He got tuberculosis, which in those days, was pretty much a death sentence. He died in Rome at the age of 25."

"Wow! That's young. And tragic, especially since that's something that can be cured today."

"Yes! When he knew he was dying, legend says he asked his friends to put this on his tombstone: 'Here lies one whose name was writ in water.'"

"Hmmm. What does that mean?"

"Here," Addie said, indicating the pool of water next to them. "Write my name in this water."

"What? Really?"

"Yes, try it."

Joshua leaned over on his elbow next to the pool and extended the index finger of his other hand. He began to write the letter 'A,' but no sooner than he do so, it swirled away in the water.

"You see? It didn't last," Addie explained. "It's just like life was for Keats; it was over way too soon."

"Gone too soon, like a lot of the guys who died in 'Nam," Joshua added. "I have to admit, though, that is kind of creepy thing to dwell on."

"I suppose, but if you think about it, life goes by too quickly anyway, whether you die at 25 or 85. My take-away is that we need to live life to the fullest. As the Romantics said, 'Carpe diem! Live for today.' I don't mean living to party, like Byron and Shelly did. I mean, we should strive to make a difference while we can. Be the best we can be."

A breeze picked up suddenly, and Joshua felt a chill. And with that chill, he also felt a strange premonition, one he dismissed quickly. The day was too beautiful, too perfect for thinking like that. Reaching over to Addie, he grasped her hand and smiled. She squeezed his hand and smiled right back.

"That's deep, Addie. I hope we have time to make a difference. Maybe even together."

"Me, too."

CHAPTER NINE
The Verdict Is In

It may have been Joshua's imagination, but it seemed as though everything got much quieter as they glided up to the dock. Maybe it was just the quiet after cutting the engine, but the silence was eerie. Sabrina, Scott, and Joshua fixed their eyes upon the detective like people who were facing their executioner. For his part, the detective gazed at them impassively. With an almost imperceptible nod of his head towards the upper part of the dock, he invited them to join him there, and then he turned and walked away. As the trio followed Detective Dupont, Greg and Shelly wisely stayed behind to stow the gear on the boat. Once the trio reached the top of the dock, he spoke.

"I felt like I owed you an explanation, and it seemed best to do it in private. In fact, I thought you should be the first to know."

"Quit beating around the bush," Scott exploded. "What's going on?"

"We got the results back from the ballistics test."

Sabrina gasped and then held her breath. Addressing her, the detective said, "Your pistol was not the murder weapon." Sabrina exhaled loudly and leaned into Scott.

"So, what happens next?" Joshua asked.

"What happens next is that I go back to work," the detective replied. "Just because your pistol was not the murder weapon doesn't mean you are in the clear," he said, looking intently at Sabrina. Then, looking at Scott, he added, "Or you, either. Maybe we just haven't found the right .22. On the other hand, maybe there are others I need to interview," he said, giving Joshua a meaningful look. With that, he turned and walked to his car.

The group was stunned to silence.

**

After the confrontation, Joshua figured Scott and Sabrina needed some space. Monday was not a normal day of work for him, but they were spent, so he offered to cover for Sabrina. She happily accepted. As he prepped the bar for opening on Monday, slicing lemons and limes and wiping down tables, he came to the realization that Indian Springs had become more of a home to him than Asheville. He had friends here, fast friends, who were becoming more like family with every passing day. There truly was nothing left for him in North Carolina. He had no family there anymore, and teaching was not the same without HER. The sight of her classroom with a new teacher in it sent him over the edge. Besides, he still did not have a way home. So, he made up his mind. First thing tomorrow, he would call his principal and let him know. With that resolution made, he felt lighter, happier. He began to whistle as he wiped down the bar. No sooner had he made his decision than Mr. Joe walked in.

"Hello! Just wanted to let you know that your bus is ready. In fact, I drove it over and parked it out front. That engine is really running sweet."

Some timing, thought Joshua. "Thank you so much, Mr. Joe. Much obliged. Let me get the cash for you, so we can settle up." Retrieving his stash from the bar's safe, he paid Joe.

"Let's go have a look, Mr. Joe." It was good to see his VW again. Joshua opened the door and climbed into the seat, relishing the smell of dust and old leather. He cranked it up and listened to the sound of the new engine.

"Don't you need a ride back to your garage?" he asked Joe.

"Nah, the walk will do me good."

"Well, don't be a stranger," Joshua said, waving to Joe as he shut the door and put the bus in gear. He was happy to drive it around to the side and park it where employees parked. No more teasing from Sabrina.

Then, Joshua realized that he had his transportation back,

so he could go back to North Carolina. He wondered if this would change things. "No!" he said emphatically. "I'm not going back." He shut and locked the doors with satisfaction and returned to his place behind the bar.

Shortly thereafter, the front door opened, and Paul Scarborough walked in. Bellying up to the bar, he ordered Tequila and Lite beer in the can. Now there's a glutton for punishment, Joshua mused. Having learned from his prior experience, he alternated sips between the Tequila and the beer. Finishing the first shot, he ordered another. Joshua watched as he slowly drank the next shot, and before long, Paul's tongue loosened up as before.

"I was wondering about something. Could you take me to the place in the alley, you know, the place where...."

"OK, but are you sure that's what you want?"

"I think I do. I think I'm ready now."

Leading the way, Joshua escorted Paul through the side door into the alley. He noted with irony that he had parked his VW pretty much where Dee Dee had parked her convertible. Pointing to a place on the concrete drive, Joshua said, "She was about right there."

Paul emitted a choking sound, a repressed sob, and turned away.

"Why don't we go back inside now," Joshua offered. They turned to walk back in, but Paul stopped and stared intently into Joshua's eyes.

"I do have one question. Do you think... do you think she suffered a lot?" Paul asked, agony in his eyes.

Softly, Joshua replied, "No, I don't think so. Her face was peaceful."

Paul teared up, and Joshua couldn't help but get misty-eyed himself. He knew something about suffering and loss. The two turned slowly and re-entered the bar. As they reached the bar area, Joshua asked, "Do you want anything else?"

"No, I think I need to go home. To Haley. But thank you, thank you very much."

"No problem, Paul."

***

Joshua made the difficult call to his principal to resign. Needless to say, the school leader was not happy about the late date, but it was over now. He also contacted his landlord back in North Carolina and arranged to clean out his things at the end of August. He felt relieved, more settled, somehow, although he dreaded going back and seeing that empty house. The next item on his agenda was to share with Darnell about Paul's latest visit to the bar, and he was itching to find out what happened when the detective interviewed him. So, after he made his calls, he drove his bus to Gibson's Discount Center where he bought a new charcoal grill and some other things for his apartment. Then, he decided to invite Darnell, Mr. Frankie, and Miss Flo for steaks on Sunday. They were happy to accept.

When Sunday came, he set up his grill on the small patio outside his kitchen door. He poured in the charcoal, doused it with lighter fluid, and threw in a match. With a whoosh, it ignited. It was blazing when Darnell drove by and parked in the back.

"Do I need to call the fire department?" Darnell teased.

Joshua laughed and said, "Nah. I'm good, Triple-D."

They shook hands, and Joshua invited him in for a beer. August in the Delta is not porch-sitting weather. Instead, he had the window air conditioner cranked up high. Before long, there was a knock at his living room door, announcing that Miss Flo and Mr. Frankie had arrived. Since they lived across the hall, they didn't have far to go.

"Welcome, welcome, welcome!" Joshua said as he ushered them into the living area.

"Thanks for inviting us. Probably the first time we have been someone's guest in this big ole house," said Miss Flo.

Frankie grunted and sat down heavily on the couch. "This thing still sags," he growled.

Joshua laughed as he offered a beer to his newly arrived guests, which they happily accepted. Budweiser in the can, of course.

"So, I've got salad in the refrigerator, baked potatoes in the oven, and the rib eyes have been marinating all night."

"Sounds great!" Darnell said.

Before long, the grill was smoking and the delicious aroma of sizzling steak filled the house, even with the back door shut. Joshua manned the grill and Darnell joined him, even in the heat, while Miss Flo and Mr. Frankie relaxed inside.

"So, I've been wanting to tell you something," Joshua began. "Paul Scarborough has visited the bar a couple of times. Each time he has ordered a shot of Tequila and a Lite beer, just like Dee Dee used to do."

"Interesting."

"Yeah, especially since he obviously hates it. He is one sad sack."

"Has he said anything?"

"Nope, but the last time, he asked me to show him the spot where I found Dee Dee. And then he asked me if I thought she suffered. I told him no, and he seemed relieved, but he choked up. He's a man who has some regrets." Darnell was silent for a bit, so Joshua was forced to ask, "So, what did he say when you interviewed him?"

"Wasn't much of an interview. He insisted on meeting us off site, neither at the plant nor at the police station. We met in a cotton field off a county road."

"That's a bit unorthodox, isn't it?"

"Yeah, but the Chief made sure we 'accommodated' him, as he put it. And when we got there, his lawyer was with him. We got a steady dose of 'don't answer that!' I am getting really frustrated. I mean, it's been what, six weeks or so, and we've gotten nowhere."

"Did he at least have an alibi?"

Darnell rolled his eyes and said, "Yeah, he said he was home watching TV with Haley."

"Not much of an alibi, not really, being she is his daughter," Joshua said. "Look, let me see if I can get anything out of him. I think he trusts me, in a bartender sort of way, and he might say something to me that he wouldn't tell the police, especially all lawyered up and all."

"It's worth a try, 'cause we got nothing."

"These steaks are done. Rare, right? Let's get out of this heat and go eat!" Joshua said.

It was a hearty meal, and everyone seemed pleased with the outcome. No dessert needed, just a follow up Budweiser. As they relaxed in the living area, Joshua asked Miss Flo and Mr. Frankie to tell him the story of how they came to have a burger joint in an old gas station. He was pleased to learn more about Darnell, as well.

Miss Flo started. "My daddy Dupont owned the Sinclair Filling Station. It was full service. Daddy pumped gas, cleaned windows, and checked the oil and air pressure in the tires. He washed cars, too. He sold oil, kerosene, tires, wipers, filters, and all that plus a bunch of cigarettes, chewing tobacco, and snuff. He had cold drinks and candy bars and crackers, too."

"Man! There's nothing like that around anymore," Joshua said.

"That's right. Momma passed when I was nine, God rest her soul, so Daddy had me working the cash register after school and in the summers. Wadn't anyone else to take care of me anyhow. And then, when business was good, he hired a teenager named Joe."

"Joe, the mechanic?" Joshua asked.

"Oh, yeah. Daddy knew Joe's people, being Dupont's and all. That Joe was a born mechanic. Then, Daddy passed, and I took over. Unfortunately, I also took over his love for beer and cigarettes," she sputtered.

"Tell him how you met Uncle Frankie," Darnell volunteered.

Miss Flo laughed. "He stopped in to get gas in this rickety old truck, and it broke down before he could pull away from the pump."

"That truck was not rickety!" Mr. Frankie fumed.

"He was this skinny boy - can you believe it now? But he was good lookin'! While Joe was looking over the truck, Frankie was looking me over."

"Wuz not! You wuz lookin' me over!"

"Well, anyway, we wound up together, didn't we? Been together ever since."

"So, you and Mr. Frankie worked the station together with Joe?"

"That's right, until Joe opened his own place. And that's when this little shaver came along," Miss Flo said, pointing to Darnell. "That would have been about 1960. He showed up one day and said to me, he says, 'Miss Flo, we's family, and I need a job.'"

"Something like that," Darnell added.

"He couldn't have been more than ten. He was adorable. How could I say no? I hired him on the spot, and he stayed with us right on up 'til he got drafted for the Army. He was a great little worker. He truly became a part of our family."

"How did the place become the best cheeseburger joint in America?" asked Joshua.

"Well, something evil came to Indian Springs. It was called a 7-11. And then another, and another. We couldn't compete. So, eventually we closed. But, we saw a need. The new McDonald's was open only daylight to dark. There was nothing open for folks to eat who worked second and third shifts at the refinery. There was a 10 pm to midnight window when the shifts changed. So, Frankie starting cooking cheeseburgers."

"And the rest is history," Joshua said. "How long ya'll gonna' keep at it?"

"Well, we don't really need the money, so we could quit anytime, but then what would we do? It's who we are, I guess," Miss Flo said. "It's who we are."

"I'm glad it is, and I'm glad to know both of you," Joshua said. "And you, too, Detective Dupont. Triple-D."

Tipping his beer towards Joshua, he replied, "Mutual."

CHAPTER TEN
"On the Road Again"

He had been trying to avoid this day as long as he could, but eventually, a person must deal with reality. Reality has a way of slapping us upside the head until it has our attention, and we deal with it, Joshua mused. In his case, reality literally knocked at his door the very next day.

"Coming!" he shouted, running to the door. He opened it to find Scott standing there. "Hey, Scott. What's up?"

"Sabrina told me to come get you."

"But it's my day off. Is something wrong?"

"No. She just said you need to come."

"OK. I'll be there in a minute."

Now that he had his bus back, it didn't take long before he was facing Sabrina at the bar. "Do you need me?" he said.

"Always, but right now, I have a message for you. A man named Mr. O'Donnell called and said to call him."

Joshua knew what that meant. Mr. O'Donnell was his landlord back in North Carolina. He had a good idea what he wanted, so he dialed the number. "I guess you can take the long-distance charges out of my paycheck," he said to Sabrina.

"I guess if you're gonna' stay in town, maybe you should get a phone in your apartment."

Grinning at Sabrina, he said, "Hello? Hey, Mr. O'Donnell. This is Joshua. You needed me to call?"

"Hey, Joshua. How are you doing, son?"

"Doing fine."

"Well, we shore do miss you around here."

With a pause, Joshua said, "What can I do for you?"

"Well, Joshua, I got myself a little predicament. I know you paid your rent through the month of August, but I got someone who wants to rent it right now. Seems that the school hired this new history teacher to take your place, and since it was so last minute, she's desperate for a place to stay. She was wondering if she could move in next week on the 15th. She said she would pay you for half the month's rent."

He wanted to say that was short notice, but he had given the principal short notice himself, so he had no standing to plead that case. "Well, I would have to take off work to come up there."

"Well, here's the good part. Not only will you get half your rent plus your deposit back, but she also wants to buy some of your stuff."

"That would be a big help to me, 'cause I don't think it's worth what it would cost me to move it down here. She knows that everything is used, right? That's about all you can get on a teacher's salary."

"She does, but she doesn't have any appliances, so it would be a godsend for her. She also wants to buy the window treatments that Addie picked out. She really likes them."

He winced at the sound of Addie's name spoken so affectionately by an old friend. "OK, but what about the furniture? Does she want any of it?"

"Nah, she has her own."

"That's too bad, 'cause like I said...."

"Hey! I've got an idea," his landlord interrupted. "My wife has been after me to have a yard sale anyway, so why don't we take your furniture to my place and see if it sells? I'll give you what I can get for it."

"That would be great. That would leave just my kitchen stuff, my linens, my clothes, and my personal effects. All of which I can use. Oh yeah! And my records and record player. My bus would hold that much easily, so that would be a huge savings."

"When can you come?"

Sabrina had caught the gist of the conversation. "Well, today is your off day, and Tuesday and Wednesday are pretty slow."

"And I could go with you to help!" Scott exclaimed.

"Oh no you don't, buster! I need you here to fill in for Joshua."

"Rats! I always love road trips."

"Would you be able to get up there, get it all done, and be back in time to work Friday?" Sabrina asked.

"If I left first thing tomorrow, I could get up there. Do what needs doing on Wednesday and drive back Thursday. Sounds doable."

"OK, then," Sabrina said.

"Alright Mr. O'Donnell, I'm headed your way tomorrow."

"Sounds good! Be careful!"

"Will do!"

***

The sun was just coming up when Joshua turned onto the highway. He was staring at a ten-hour drive, and even though there was an interstate-all-the-way route, it felt out of the way to him. So, he decided to take a more scenic drive: up the Natchez Trace through Mississippi and Alabama to Tennessee; across the state to I-75; and then I-40 through Knoxville and into North Carolina. Turning on the radio, the first song playing was Willie Nelson's "On the Road Again," and he began to sing along. It did feel good to be driving again. The only downside was that he would have a lot of time to think.

The trip went well, even in the August heat. He listened to a lot of music along the way, stopping only to fill up his gas tank, go to the restroom, and grab some grub. When he finally reached his former home and pulled into the gravel driveway, a wave of sadness came over him. He was tired from the drive, but he was also filled with longing. Turning off the VW, he sighed as he surveyed the older but well-maintained little bungalow. He and Addie had some wonderful times there, but it was also where his great sadness began.

With no time to spare, he went inside and began boxing his things. It was late before he slept, but he could not bring himself to sleep in their bed. Instead, he crashed out on his couch. The sun was barely up the next day when there was a knock at his door. It was Mr. O'Donnell, holding a couple of sausage biscuits and a cup of coffee. He handed them to Joshua with a smile.

"Sarah made this special for you! It shore is good to see you! We miss you and Addie so much."

It was just this kind of conversation that Joshua dreaded. "Thank you, sir."

"Well, slurp that down and let's get started."

With Mr. O'Donnell's help, they were able to break down the furniture and, with his truck, get a lot of it moved by lunch, which was provided by Sarah O'Donnell. Fried pork chops, black-eyed peas, collard greens, green beans, and corn bread, which Joshua chased with sweet tea.

"Thank you so much, Mrs. O'Donnell! I haven't eaten this well in I don't know when."

"You are so, so welcome. So good to see you again." She could see the anguish in Joshua's eyes, so she didn't mention Addie.

That afternoon, they were able to get the rest of his things moved out, and then they loaded his VW bus. All that was left in the rental were the appliances and the curtains. Joshua sadly surveyed the empty home, his heart even more empty. With the work completed, Mr. O'Donnell invited Joshua for supper.

"No thank you, sir. You've been too good to me already. I think I'll visit the Mountain Burger for old time's sake."

"I understand. When will we see you again?"

Joshua did not know what to say, so he didn't. Instead, he dipped his head in farewell and climbed aboard his VW. He cranked it up as Mr. O'Donnell climbed into his pickup. Joshua began to back out of the driveway, but then his friend stopped and rolled down his window.

"Take care of yourself, son!" he shouted, and then he scratched gravel and began to roll down the road.

After a sleepless night in a cheap motel, Joshua pulled out

early the next morning. It was going to be a long drive back to his new home.

***

While Joshua regretted not being able to finish his planned road trip to New Orleans and the Gulf Coast, he didn't have to wait long to hear some good music. As August rolled into September, he heard about the Delta Blues Festival. This would be the fifth year of the festival, and it would be held outdoors in Freedom Village, which was near Greenville, Mississippi.

It was later in September, and a cool front had moved through, breaking up the humidity, which was a blessed relief. Scott and Sabrina, along with Greg and Shelly, piled into the VW bus on Sunday to head to Freedom Village, about an hour and fifteen minutes away. Their cooler was stocked with beer, water, ice, and food, although they hoped to find some good barbecue at the festival. They also brought lawn chairs.

"So, Scott, have you decided on a fall play?" Greg asked as they puttered along the highway.

"Wow! Look at all that cotton," Joshua exclaimed at the white fields stretching to the horizon. "Oh, sorry, Greg."

"Well, I like the *Odd Couple* idea a lot, but we would have to have two really strong actors experienced in comedy," he replied. "Just not sure we have that. On the other hand, Shelly could make a really good Corie in *Barefoot in the Park*."

"Like the sound of that!" Shelly replied.

"We would just need someone to play her husband Paul."

"How much experience would such an actor need?" Sabrina asked, nodding her head towards Joshua.

Joshua did not miss her nod or its implication. "You can forget about that!" he stated firmly.

"I don't know. You've got those Robert Redford good looks," she said.

Joshua blushed and then burst out laughing. "Now I know how you suckered Jeff into playing Stanley in *Streetcar*. Why don't you ask him?"

"Jeff was great, but I'm not sure he's right for the part.

Besides, he told me that he wanted to spend some time coaching his son in youth football this fall," Scott said.

"You know, there is someone who might pull it off," Sabrina suggested. "A teacher at the high school named Michael Hudson."

"Who is that?" Greg asked.

"He's an English teacher," Scott said. "I think he did some shows in college at Millsaps."

"Well, he doesn't have family here, so he might be available," Sabrina said.

"I need to check that out. If we are going to do a fall show, we need to get started soon," said Scott.

"Changing the subject," Sabrina directed towards Joshua, "but a little birdie told me that you and Detective Dupont have become buddies."

"Yeah, I guess you could say that."

"What do you two have in common?" she asked.

"What do you and your 'little birdies,' Jeff and Reuben, have in common?" he countered.

"Touche'."

"Actually, we both served in the Army," Joshua said.

"Ah, OK. Let me ask you something then," Sabrina said. Joshua winced. Please don't let it be about Vietnam, he prayed. She asked wistfully, "Has he let you in on anything? Any new developments?"

"Not really.... for suspects, I mean. It's starting to turn into a little bit of a cold case."

"Did he ever talk to Paul, Dee Dee's husband?"

"I would imagine he did," Joshua hedged, being careful what he revealed.

"I can't help but think he had to have had something to do with it," Sabrina said. "Either him or her ex."

"Speaking of her ex, have you ever met him?" Joshua asked.

"I think he came into the bar once this summer. You might have been off that night. Anyway, he is a piece of work.

Scruffy beard, greasy hair in a ponytail, feed cap. Plaid western shirt, big cowboy belt buckle, and cowboy boots. Strutting around like he was a stud." Joshua huffed. "I overheard him running his mouth about how he was going to get custody of Haley now that Dee Dee was dead, but that sorry husband of hers was standing in the way. Now there's a motive for murder."

"Maybe," Joshua admitted, reluctant to reveal more, even though he knew Darnell found out the ex- had an alibi for the night Dee Dee died. "I wonder why he couldn't get custody anyway?"

"I heard he had too many run-ins with the law and smoked too much grass."

The conversation was interrupted by Scott as he pointed out the sign to the festival entrance. Turning in, the crew was amazed at what they found. The tickets were very inexpensive, and there was plenty of parking. The entire venue was contained in a large soybean field that had been harvested. The sun was bright, and the cloudless sky was a deep blue. Peavey Sound, a Mississippi company who was famous for their amps and speakers, oversaw the sound, and they set up towers of speakers around the field, so everyone could hear clearly. There was no annoying blast of sound from the center stage. The group was also surprised that they would be able to set up relatively near the bands.

The first big act was John Lee Hooker. They couldn't help but get up and dance to "Boogie Chillen," but when he launched into "Boom Boom," the audience was on fire. With a break between sets, they set out looking for barbecue ribs. What they found did not disappoint. They were served what was called a "rib sandwich." It was not a sandwich in the true sense: what it was, was a giant slab of ribs that had been slow-cooked over hickory chips. It was served over four slices of white bread, which were drowning in sauce. The sauce was sweet and tangy, but there was a little heat to it, also. The idea was to dip the ribs in the sauce and then sop up the remaining sauce with the bread.

As they sat at a picnic table outside the rib shack, Joshua

licked his lips and said, "I have never tasted anything like this!"

Scott replied with something that sounded like, "Mumpha mumph mumph." Too busy eating to talk.

"It just falls right off the bone!" Greg said. "Different taste than St. Louis barbecue, but man, it is good!"

"Pretty messy, though," Sabrina said.

"Good thing they put a roll of paper towels on the table!" said Shelly.

After they laid waste to the ribs, they wandered back to their lawn chairs to hear more blues. Next up was the legendary Muddy Waters. He cranked up the crowd with "Hoochie Coochie Man." His set ended with the famous song "Mannish Boy." The whole crowd sang along to the lyrics: "I'm A Man... M chile... A chile... N chile...."

The sun was beginning to set as they loaded up their stuff to head home. Looking back over the scene and relishing the day, Joshua said, to no one in particular, "Addie would have loved this!"

"Who's Addie?" Sabrina asked.

Joshua's face said he had slipped up and let out some big secret. "That's a story for another day," he said quietly.

Sabrina and Scott gave each other a puzzled look before they boarded the bus. Joshua fired up the engine, and they headed back to Indian Springs to the sounds of Joshua's new Muddy Waters cassette.

CHAPTER ELEVEN
Revelations and Invitations

Tuesday night rolled around way too soon, and Joshua found himself manning the bar by himself. It wasn't long before Scott bounced in through the dressing room door, plopped down on a stool, and ordered a Coors Lite. As Joshua reached into the beer cooler under the counter, he asked, "Did ya'll ever decide on which play you will do for the fall?"

Taking a sip of his icy beer, Scott replied, "Yeah. We decided to do *Barefoot in the Park.* Shelly will play the female romantic lead, Corie, and Michael Hudson, the teacher at the high school, has agreed to do the male romantic lead, her husband Paul."

"Good!"

"I scored again! I also got a retired English teacher from Choctaw County High School to play Corie's mother. She has done a lot of theater, and she's perfect for that role."

"Sounds promising!"

"Yes, but the best score is that I got a big local name to play the eccentric neighbor, Mr. Velasco. He's the guy that Corie tries to set her mother up with. Drumroll, please?"

"Just pretend you are hearing it. Who is it?"

"I got the mayor to do that part. He is very popular and well-known. He will draw a big crowd."

"Sounds good. When do you start rehearsals?"

"We are going to do our read-through Thursday night and start blocking next Monday."

"So, when will it debut?"

"First week in November. That will give us six weeks of rehearsal, which should be enough."

"Didn't you say the play takes place in New York City?

Greg is great with sets, but how is he going to pull that off?"

"Most of the show takes place in the young married couple's apartment, so that should be fairly easy. Greg said something about projecting images and stuff. I don't know. I'm sure he will figure it out."

"I'm sure Greg will do a great job."

"Speaking of Greg, I'm supposed to be meeting with him right now, so I'd better split!" Scott set his empty beer down on the bar and hustled out. He threw up his hand and waved over his shoulder as he shut the dressing room door.

The night drug along after that. Very slow, even for a Tuesday. And then, when it was almost closing time, the door opened, and Paul Scarborough walked in.

"Do you want the usual?" Joshua asked as Paul sat at the bar.

"Hmmmm. You know what? I think I'm done with tequila and Lite Beer. I've done my penance. How 'bout you pour me some Old Charter, Ten Year-Old, neat."

"Sure thing!" Joshua said, wondering what he meant by "penance."

As Joshua turned to fetch a glass and the bottle of whiskey, Paul added, "Make that a double!" Joshua obliged and set the drink on the bar. Paul sipped on it thoughtfully, and Joshua slipped away for a minute to take care of the trash and do some restocking. When he returned, Paul was leaning on the jukebox, trying to decide what he should play.

"Do you remember what Dee Dee liked to listen to?" he asked.

"Uh, I seem to remember she liked 'Looking for Love.'"

A strained look passed across Paul's face, but he put a quarter in and punched the number for that song. As it began to play, he returned to the bar, empty glass in hand. "Hit me again, barkeep," he intoned. As Joshua placed the drink on the bar, he noticed that the music had a strange effect on Paul. He became maudlin very quickly. And then, he downed the double. Joshua wondered if Paul could keep it together.

"Hit me again!" Paul slurred.

"Sure thing, but I believe this is gonna' be last call. Hey, do they have taxis in Indian Springs?"

Paul started to object, but he thought better of it. Instead, he played with the glass for a minute before he took a sip. "You know what I liked about Dee Dee the most? Dee Dee had this spirit about her, this zest for life." Joshua just listened, like a seasoned bartender.

"I mean," Paul continued, taking another sip, "she went through hell as a kid. Then, raising Haley as a single parent, working her butt off to support her. But she never complained. She always had a smile on her face, and she was always ready to celebrate life!"

"That's quite a tribute, Paul."

"Yes, well, she was quite a woman. I miss her. Bad. And it's all my fault that she's gone."

Joshua's ears perked up. "What do you mean?"

The question startled Paul, and he began to hem and haw as though he knew he had said too much. Then, suddenly, he said, "You know what. You are right. I've had enough. See you later!" Leaving his drink on the bar, he lowered himself gingerly from his stool and began to wobble towards the door.

"Hey, Paul! You OK to drive, buddy?"

"Sure, sure," he said, and the door banged shut behind him.

Joshua did not know what to make of Paul's statements. Penance? A confession, maybe? Regardless, he had something to tell Darnell the next time he saw him.

***

"Miss Flo, anybody here? Ya'll open?" Joshua called out in the empty diner.

"Of course we are open," Miss Flo replied, appearing from the kitchen. "Haven't seen you around here in a while."

"Sorry about that. I've been busy settling my business, here and in North Carolina.

"Well, we're just glad you are staying. You want a beer and

a burger?"

"Yes, ma'am!"

"Well, you know the drill. FRANKIE!" she bellowed.

"Coming right up," he yelled in reply.

It wasn't long before Darnell appeared with a juicy burger and a pile of fries.

"You not eating, Triple-D?"

"I ate earlier. Good to see you, my friend."

"Good to see you. Hey, I gotta' know. How do you always know I'm here, and how do you get here so fast?"

"Ah, that's my little secret. Let's just say I have my sources."

"Sure, Miss Flo and Mr. Frankie. But how do you get here so quickly? You must live, like, right around the corner."

"I guess you could say that."

"C'mon. Out with it."

"OK. I'll let you in on it. When I finished up at Jackson State and got the job here, Auntie Flo and Uncle Frankie insisted they set me up with a place to live."

"So why aren't you living in the house with us?"

"Well, they knew they could rent those apartments, but what they couldn't rent was the garage space that's attached to the diner. So, they took everything out, cleaned up the place, and remodeled it for me. It is now a nice little apartment."

"So, you literally live right next door!" Joshua said and laughed.

"Right. With a connecting door. And now, they have a built-in alarm system: me, a cop living here."

"Well, I'll be! That's pretty cool. You will have to show me the place sometime. Hey, before I forget, there is a little tip I wanted to pass along to you. Paul stopped by the bar the other night."

Darnell's eyes widened and he leaned in to hear.

"First, he talked about penance. And then, after he had a few drinks, he got sad, especially after playing Dee Dee's favorite song on the jukebox And then he said something strange. He said that it was all his fault. Meaning her death. I didn't know what to make of that."

"Hmmm. Not exactly a confession, but he knows something he's not saying. There's something going on that we just can't put our fingers on."

"Can you lean on him?"

"I would love to, but between the mayor and his lawyer, not sure that I can pull that off. What was your sense of it?"

"To be honest, I believe he really loved Dee Dee, admired her even. I don't know if I see him killing her out of jealousy, even in a fit of rage. Still, he's connected to it somehow. The guilt just rolls off him."

"Well, keep your ears open, barkeep. You might hear more. In the meantime, I'm going to do some more sniffing around Paul. His business dealings, his personal life. Who knows what might turn up."

"Will do!" Joshua said, as he stood up to leave. "Oh, speaking of his personal life. This may not mean anything, but Scott told me that Paul really likes to gamble. He actually met Dee Dee at the Choctaw Reservation Casino, he said."

"Hmmm. That's something to think about, for sure."

"Hey, Joshua!' called out Miss Flo, as she walked in, wiping her hands on her apron. "Now that you are settled in and all and living amongst us, I wanted to invite you to church. We have our service at 11. Why don't you come next Sunday?"

"Where do ya'll go to church?"

"It's a little church out in the country, right off the main highway. The Church of the Lost and Found."

Interesting name, Joshua thought. "Thank you, ma'am, for the invitation," he said.

"Come see us. I mean it," she said sweetly. "Listen. I'm not trying to convert you or anything. I just get this feeling that you are carrying a heavy load." Joshua gulped. "They shore helped me when I lost my mother and father. Maybe our little church is a place where you can lay your burden down. If I might be so bold, maybe you can find a way to forgive yourself."

Joshua was stunned at how easily she saw into his heart. "That's something to think about," he stuttered as he turned to the door, his eyes tearing up. "See ya'll again soon!"

"Don't be a stranger!" she called after him.

***

Saturday night came, and Joshua and Sabrina were both working the bar. The Mindbenders were playing for a big crowd, celebratory even. Ole Miss had just won a big football game, so the crowd was ready to party. The two barkeeps served lots of beer and lots of Jack Daniels and Coke. Football drinks.

When the band took a break, someone in the crowd started a cheer. "Hotty Toddy, Gosh Almighty, Who the Hell are we? Flim, flam; bim, bam! Ole Miss by damn!" Before long, everyone joined in, and the rafters shook.

"Don't think I've ever heard a cheer like that," Joshua said, shaking his head.

"It was new to me when we first got here, but I was told it's the signature cheer for Ole Miss. Supposedly, it goes back to the early 1900's."

"What does it mean?"

"Nobody really knows. It's even the official greeting between Ole Miss fans," Sabrina added.

"Who's the guy who started it? He sort of stood out with his college frat boy look, especially since he looks a lot older than a college kid."

The fellow that Joshua indicated was clearly the center of attention for a large part of the crowd, leading them in laughter like the Pied Piper. Early forties, nice-looking, but in a too-much-partying, washed-out sort of way. He wore madras print Bermuda shorts, a starched white oxford cloth button down with sleeves rolled up, and a pair of oxblood-colored loafers with tassles, no socks.

"I don't know him," Sabrina replied. "Remember, I haven't been in town much longer than you. He's not a regular, that's for sure. Need to ask another regular, I guess."

"The Mississippi Delta sure is an interesting place," Joshua said.

***

After the second blocking rehearsal the following Tuesday night, Scott and some of the cast members came down for a drink. Scott had a suspicious look on his face.

"Uh, Joshua, I need your help," he began.

Warning bells began to sound in Joshua's mind. "No Coors Lite first?" he joked, trying to sense which way the wind was blowing.

"Yeah, sure. Thanks."

Joshua served the drink and then tried to find something else to do. He had a feeling where this was going.

"So, yeah, Joshua. Here's the thing. I'm one actor short, and I was wondering if you might consider...."

"No, I don't think so."

"C'mon, man! It's a short part. No lines even."

"I don't think so. I'm not an actor. I'm not used to getting up in front of a crowd."

"Now that's where I'm gonna' call 'bull!'" Scott exclaimed. "Weren't you a teacher?"

"Well, yeah, but what has that got to do with it?"

"How many kids did you get up in front of a day?"

"I don't know. Maybe 120 to 130." Joshua did not like where this was going.

"And did you read your lectures from a script, or did you just know the material?"

"I learned it."

"Well, that sounds like a performance to me, bub!" Joshua was stumped. He felt the vultures circling. Scott could tell he had him on the ropes. "Like I said, small part, no lines."

With dread in his voice, Joshua asked, "What's the part?"

"It's just the bellhop, at the beginning of the show. You carry the honeymooners' luggage into their room, and after that, you bring them their paper. A little bit of physical comedy, but no biggie."

"I don't know, man."

"OK, I didn't want to play this card, but you owe me."

"What do you mean?"

"Who rescued you from sleeping in your bus and let you sleep in a real bed in the theater?"

Joshua felt cornered, trapped.

"Please?"

Joshua had one last excuse. "But who covers the bar for me when we rehearse, and especially during the show?"

"Oh, that's easy. We'll only need you to rehearse a little. Monday nights when you are off. And during the play, like I said, your bit takes place at the very beginning of the show. Sabrina can cover that and then you come down through the dressing room to go back to work."

He sighed. "Is there absolutely no one else?"

"Just you, and you are perfect for the part!"

Joshua's stomach was already knotting up.

CHAPTER TWELVE
"Time Flies When You're Having Fun"

The weeks during rehearsal passed quickly, too quickly for Joshua, and now he stood backstage, a knot in his stomach. It was opening night for *Barefoot in the Park.* He thought he looked ridiculous in his bellboy "monkey suit" and grease paint on his face. Sweat trickled down his back and slid down his cheek. And suddenly, the curtain began to roll back. Show time!

Joshua stumbled a bit as he began to walk downstage center to the door of the couple's honeymoon suite, a suitcase in each hand. The audience had their eye on the young newlyweds, who trailed behind him arm in arm, but Joshua felt like the searchlight of God was on him and him alone. He set the suitcases down, unlocked the door, and then carried their luggage inside, which was behind the curtain. The amorous young couple shared their lines, and then Joshua returned. The actor playing Paul tipped him, and Joshua the bellhop tipped his cap to the couple, before departing downstage left.

Paul swept Corie up in his arms and carried her inside, kicking the door shut with his foot. Three beats later, he reopened the door and hung a do not disturb sign. Another three beats, and Joshua walked by and dropped the next morning's newspaper beside the door, before exiting. He quickly made his way behind the curtain and then hurried backstage to downstage left again. He then walked to the couple's door with another newspaper, which he dropped. Rinse and repeat, but this time, the hapless bellboy noticed that the papers had not been touched. Joshua faced the audience and gave them a big, theatrical shrug of the shoulders before walking offstage, laughter at the sight gag in his wake. His part was done. Thank God! Time to change downstairs and resume his job behind the bar, much to his relief.

The show went well, and Joshua gradually got over his stage fright. By the time the Sunday matinee rolled around, he felt like a veteran. Even Darnell came to that performance, and Joshua made a special point to invite him to the cast party.

Bellying up to the bar, Darnell teased, "What's up, 'Hollywood'?"

"Alright now, Triple-D."

"I don't know if I can stand to be in the presence of such a big-time celebrity as you."

Joshua laughed and said, "Do you want a beer or not?"

"Sure. Give me a Bud draft but sign my napkin first."

"Dude! Come on! Do you want this drink or not?!"

Sabrina gave Detective Dupont and Joshua a cautious look, as she served a couple of Chardonnays to Greg and Shelly at the other end of the bar. Then came a roar of laughter from the center of the room, drawing everyone's eyes to His Honor the Mayor, who held court, surrounded by his admirers. Darnell turned his eyes from the mayor back to Joshua and gave an exaggerated eye roll.

"Not a fan?" Joshua teased.

"As they say in Washington, 'No comment!'"

"Probably a good idea," Joshua conceded, as Scott stepped up for a drink.

"Scott, I believe you did really well casting the Mayor as Victor the neighbor," said Joshua.

"Thanks! We actually set records for attendance at each performance."

"Nice," Joshua said.

Directing his attention to Scott, Darnell said, "Well, congratulations, Mr. Director, Sir."

"Ah, well, thanks officer," Scott replied uncomfortably.

Sabrina joined the trio, swallowed and said, "Nice to see you taking in a show, uh, ah...."

Jeff and Reuben crowded up to the bar to join the group. Soon, they were debating the best parts of the play. They agreed that Michael Hudson, the teacher at the local high school, had done very well as the uptight lawyer Paul, but Shelly stole the show as the irrepressible Corie.

"And there she is, the star of the show," Scott crowed as Greg and Shelly walked over.

"Thanks, guys, but everyone was great."

"Greg, you outdid yourself this time with those sets," Joshua said.

"Seriously," Scott began, "the idea of leaving the scrim down and projecting the outer wall of the brownstone on it was genius. Then, by switching from front-lighting to back-lighting, the walls appeared to melt away, so we could see inside the apartment. Then, it was easy work to raise the scrim. Good stuff!"

"Not sure we could have pulled off a brownstone any other way," Greg replied modestly.

"Hey, where is Michael Hudson?" Sabrina asked.

"He said he had to go down to Jackson to check on his folks. I hope everything is OK," Scott said.

Eventually the party began to wind down, at about the same pace as the free alcohol and food disappeared. With few people left in the bar, Joshua had an opportunity to talk with Darnell about the case of Dee Dee Scarborough.

"So, Darnell. Have you learned anything about Paul yet?"

"Well, the easy part was finding that he has no criminal record. Other than that, it's hard to find out specifics without a subpoena. Still, I have some sources that at least gave me a better picture. Some guys who work at the refinery are regulars at Auntie Flo and Uncle Frankie's. They say that Paul is OK to work for. Not a pain in the butt, like some bosses have been in the past. They say he's a straight-up dude, very level-headed."

"Go on," Joshua encouraged.

"I was able to talk to some of Dee Dee's friends, off the record, and they said that Dee Dee never said anything bad about Paul. They saw no evidence of mistreatment, or anything like that, either. He seemed to them like he really loved Dee Dee and

Haley, and she really cared for him."

"Not surprised at that."

"My connection at the bank couldn't give me any specifics, but they were able to tell me that he pays his bills, keeps up his line of credit, and is not in debt any more than the average Joe in his financial bracket."

"What about his gambling? Find out anything about that?"

"Well, I have a friend who's an officer over near the Casino. He poked around a little bit for me and gave me what he could find out. Apparently, Paul did like to gamble, and that is in fact where he met Dee Dee. However, I couldn't find anything that would connect him to her murder from that connection. And, I found out that the casino is a pretty straight-forward deal."

"What do you mean?"

"Well, as you know, gambling is illegal in the state, but their land is federal land, so the Choctaw got an exemption."

"Humph! I'm surprised that the Cherokee back in North Carolina haven't tried the same thing," Joshua said.

"They probably will, eventually. Anyway, the Choctaw know that they have ta' keep it squeaky clean to keep their exemption. They make a lot of money for their people, so they are very motivated to run it right. And before you ask, doesn't sound like there are mob connections like you hear about in Vegas or New Jersey."

"So, that sounds like a dead end."

"Yeah, but it is interesting how it works when you gamble there."

"What do you mean?"

"Well, big gamblers like Paul can use a line of credit from their bank to get chips. What the big boys do is get no more than $9,000 a pop, because you have to report anything ten grand or more to the IRS. My connection found out that, unofficially, Paul was one of the bigger gamblers, but it sounded like he stayed in the black somehow. At any rate, if he owed a bunch of money, it would be to the bank. Like I said before, the bank said he was on track there."

"Hmmmm. I guess you would have to break even to gamble as much as he did. He may be the plant's boss, and one of the more well-off guys in town, but he doesn't make the kind of money a body would need to gamble the way he does. Unless he had a kindly uncle or a stash we don't know about."

"So, what's your take now, barkeep? Still think he loved Dee Dee and had nothing to do with her murder?"

"I think he really did love her, and I don't know that he killed her, but I can't shake this feeling that it's all connected to him somehow. At least he thinks so."

"Well, it's going on five months now since she died, and the trail is getting colder and colder," Darnell remarked glumly.

"There is something I found out a while back about Dee Dee's ex-," Joshua began, "but I didn't bring it up because I didn't figure it mattered. It seems that after Dee Dee died, her ex- was in the bar bragging about getting custody of Haley. A custody dispute gone bad? That could lead to murder."

"True, but like I told you before, he has an alibi."

"Yeah, I remember you telling me that. That's why I didn't think it would matter, but it's always good to have all the facts, anyway. Well, partner, I hate to say it, but it's about time to shut this party down and close up. As they say, 'Closing time! You don't have to go home, but you can't stay here.'"

"Roger that, my friend," Darnell said, as he hopped off his bar stool and headed for the door.

"Good seeing you, Triple-D," Joshua said, as Darnell waved over his shoulder.

***

It didn't take long for the "high" of the play to wear off. All it took was for Shannon Newcombe to flounce into the bar the Tuesday after. In what she thought was a seductive walk, the reporter sauntered to the bar with a wide grin on her face.

Crap! Joshua thought. Sabrina walked in from the restaurant next door, and upon seeing the stranger, had a puzzled expression on her face.

"What'll ya' have?" Joshua asked.

"What, you don't remember me?" she asked.

"Oh yeah, you're that TV reporter."

"That's right. From Channel Six in Greenwood."

"So, I'll ask again. What do you want?"

"What I want and what I need are two different things," she replied. "What I need is to speak with Sabrina Goodman."

Sabrina's eyes widened. "What do you want with her?" she asked.

"Well, that's between me and her."

"Hunh! Well, you just missed her. She's not here right now," Sabrina fibbed.

"Well, that's odd. I was told she was working tonight."

"Somebody told you wrong!" Sabrina said sarcastically.

"Well, do me a favor. When you see her, give her my card." She slipped her business card on the bar and shoved it towards Sabrina. "I want to talk to her about the murder of Dee Dee Scarborough. I have it on good authority that she is the leading suspect." Ignoring the astonished look on Sabrina's face, Newcombe whirled around and strutted out of the bar, leaving the door ajar behind her.

"Oh my God! Can you believe this!" Sabrina yelped.

Joshua didn't know what to say. This was a very unexpected development. He could feel the frustration and sadness emanating from Sabrina, as tears slid down her cheek.

"When is your *friend* Darnell gonna' find the real killer, so people will just LEAVE. ME. ALONE!" she shouted as she banged through the theater's dressing room door.

Don't know how much more of this she can take, Joshua mused.

***

Unlike Fall in North Carolina, the weather in the Delta was much more moderate in November. As Joshua wiped down the bar at The Boiler Room, he was wondering if Winter would also be as mild. His thoughts were soon interrupted.

"JOSHUA!"

He looked up just in time to see Carly Jane Lacy weaving through the crowd waving at him.

"Hey, Carly Jane, what can I get you?"

"Well, since you don't have what I really want.... You know the rest," she said and laughed.

"Right. A Jack and Coke for you, and four Bud Lites for the boys in the band. Except the band is not playing tonight. Oh, but look! They're here." Joshua winked at her and nodded to the boys. "Coming right up."

Flipping her blonde hair out of her eyes, she asked, "Hey, Joshua. Has anyone told you about the Hunting Club Party?"

"Don't think so."

"Yeah, well, deer season opens on Thanksgiving Day, so they always have this big party the Saturday night after. All the beer and barbecue deer ribs you can eat for a $5 donation. They have, like, this massive Quonset hut, slash tractor barn that they hold it in. And the Mindbenders will be playing."

"Sounds like fun."

"Well, you should come!"

"Don't you have to be a hunter to go?"

She giggled and said, "Do I look like a hunter to you?"

"Guess not, but don't you have to be invited?"

"Well, I'm inviting you as a guest of the band."

"OK then, give me the date, and I'll see if I can get the night off."

"Sure thing!" she said, as she turned to take the beer to the boys. She held her drink in one hand and the four long necks between the fingers of her other hand.

"She would make a good bartender," Joshua said to Sabrina.

"Yeah, but we would run out of Jack," Sabrina deadpanned.

***

Before he knew it, it was Thanksgiving week. Miss Flo invited Joshua for Thanksgiving lunch with Mr. Frankie and

Darnell, and he gladly accepted. When he knocked on the door of Miss Flo's apartment, it was opened almost immediately by Mr. Frankie.

"Just so you know, don't be expecting any turkey today. Too hard to find a good one and too expensive. Not to mention that meat is so dry!"

"Well, whatever you are making, it sure smells good in here!" Joshua replied.

Miss Flo took up the banter as Joshua entered the room. "Don't you worry, honey. Auntie Flo knows how to make a delicious baking hen. The meat is much more tender and juicy. And yes, we'll still have cornbread dressing, giblet gravy, and cranberry sauce. You might like my deviled eggs, too."

"Yes, ma'am. Thanks so much for inviting me."

"Well, go on in the living room with Darnell. He's watching the parade on TV. Leave the cooking to me and Uncle Frankie." Darnell was flopped out on the couch so thoroughly, that Joshua decided to take a chair.

"Mornin'," Darnell muttered sleepily. "You know what I like about Turkey Day? Don't have to talk business." He looked at Joshua pointedly.

"Gotcha." Joshua had the feeling that Darnell did not want to talk about the murder of Dee Dee Scarborough on this, of all days.

They settled in to watch the Macy's Thanksgiving Day Parade. Bryant Gumbel was one of the hosts, and he chattered away with some lady co-host that Joshua didn't recognize. He recognized the giant balloons, though. Mickey Mouse, Snoopy, Underdog, the Cat in the Hat, the Smurfs, and Bullwinkle the Moose. The Rockettes were there, as well as Debbie Allen's dancers from *Fame.* Laura Branigan sang her hit "Gloria," and even the Muppets made an appearance. Before long, Miss Flo announced that lunch was ready.

And what a feast it was. Not only the hen and dressing, which were mouth-watering, but homemade yeast rolls, green beans, black-eyed peas, lima beans, sweet potato casserole, and mashed potatoes. The giblet gravy was mighty fine over the potatoes, as well over the dressing. And for dessert - Pecan Pie, of course.

After finishing his feast, Joshua pushed back from the table with a sigh. "As good as it was, I don't think I can take another bite."

"Just wait a while," Darnell said, "and you might be ready for more."

"I don't know."

"Well, honey, if you are not, you can sure take some home with you!" Miss Flo said.

Joshua offered to help clean up, but Miss Flo wouldn't have it. The men retreated to the living room to watch football. The New York Giants were playing the Detroit Lions. Joshua was not sure when he nodded off, but he was awakened by Darnell yelling as Lawrence Taylor intercepted the ball and returned it for the winning touchdown. Giants 13, Lions 6.

All in all, a great day. Joshua was happy that he had someone to spend Thanksgiving with. As he walked across the hall to his apartment, loaded down with containers of food, he couldn't help but remember his last Thanksgiving with Addie. She would have loved these people, and she would have loved this day. He unlocked his door with a sigh.

CHAPTER THIRTEEN
It Wouldn't Be a Party Without a Fight

Joshua managed to get the bar covered for the Saturday after Thanksgiving, so he went to the Hunting Club party. Carly Jane gave him directions, and they were not hard to follow - at first. Down the hill from his apartment, through Indian Springs, across the Choctaw River Bridge, and then a right on River Road. That was the easy part, as the road paralleled the river. The hard part was finding the correct dirt road, among the scores of them, on which to turn in the dark. The longer he drove, the more he felt like he was entering a jungle in 'Nam, as the lights of his VW illuminated swamps and trees. After one or two misses, Joshua found the right road, and he began to see the lights from the big tractor barn up ahead. Parking along the side of the dirt road next to a barbed wire fence, he locked his bus and began to walk to the gate.

It wasn't long before Joshua could hear the distinctive sound of the Mindbenders as he crunched through the gravel. It was a chilly November night, and he flipped up the collar on his army field jacket and stuck his hands in the pockets. The cold wind ensured that he had his five dollars ready when he got to the gate. Making his way into the large barn, the warmth welcomed him. He quickly noticed that the heat was produced by coal burning in steel drums that were scattered around the huge barn. Smoky, but effective. There were at least two or three kegs of beer operational, and a line of tables covered in barbecue deer ribs beckoned. The Mindbenders were pumping out the sound - the Beach Boys - and folks were dancing and milling around together in a roiling mass in front of the stage. Joshua secured a draft beer in a red Solo cup and sipped it as he surveyed the crowd.

"Joshua!" a familiar voice cried. "Glad you made it!" Carly Jane exclaimed in his ear.

"Only one or two wrong turns," he said with a grin.

"Have you eaten any ribs yet?"

"Nah. Just got here."

"They are scrumptious. You gotta' get some."

"I've always heard they taste pretty gamey."

"Not if you prepare them right," Carly Jane said. "Wait. You mean you've never had venison before? A North Carolina boy?"

"Well, believe it or not, we don't have a lot of deer in North Carolina. They were pretty much hunted out by the early settlers. Any deer up there now were introduced from somewhere else by park rangers. So, how do they get that bloody taste out anyway?"

"There are different ways. Some people say that you have to bleed the deer quickly after you shoot it. Other folks say cut out all the fat, which is where the gamey taste comes from. Other people say soak 'em."

"What do you soak 'em in?"

"Some people use buttermilk, some folks use salt water, and some people use vinegar water. Then, you slow cook them on low heat in an oven. After they are done, throw them on the grill with barbecue sauce to give it the right taste."

"Sounds good," Joshua said.

"Well, let's try some, then!"

Joshua and Carly Jane grabbed a paper plate each and forked out some ribs. Trying a bite, he said, "Not bad. Not bad at all."

"They are good!"

"I can still taste a little gaminess, if there is such a word, but they are pretty good. Not quite as tender as pork ribs, but not bad."

Giggling, she said, "Well, they sure go better with draft beer!"

Just as Joshua took a large bite, he saw her, as if she were haunting him. But at least this time he knew it was only "The

Noodle Princess." He was not going to let this opportunity pass; he had to meet her.

"Excuse me, Carly Jane. I need to go talk to someone."

"No problem. Have fun!"

Joshua cautiously approached the young woman who looked so much like Addie. She was sipping her beer and swaying to the music. "Excuse me," he said.

"Oh, hey," she said.

"I just wanted to meet you. My name is Joshua. Joshua MacMillian."

"Well, hey there," she replied. "I'm Jessica. Jessica Greenhaw."

"Hey, Jessica. Uh, I don't want you to take this wrong, but I've seen you around a couple of times, and you look just like someone I used to know." Her eyes widened at that remark, and that is when Joshua realized that she had green eyes, not deep, almost black ones, like Addie. Other than that, she could have been her sister: dark complexion and dark hair in twin French braids. Same height and build, just younger.

When she looked over her shoulder for a way to escape the conversation, Joshua realized that a thirty-two-year-old guy like him talking to an eighteen-year-old girl might seem a bit creepy, so he hastened to say, "I know that sounds like a dumb pick-up line or something, but I promise that is not why I'm talking to you. The person you look like was very special to me, and I..., I lost her. You just remind me of her, that's all."

She seemed to relax and then said, "I think I've seen you before. Don't you work at the Boiler Room?"

"Yeah, that's me."

"And, I think I saw you one time at the lake," she added.

"Yep, passing by on a pontoon boat. I remember."

"OK, well nice to meet you, Joshua."

"I do have a question. Are you part Native-American? My friend was."

"Yep, one quarter Choctaw, three quarters mutt," she said and laughed.

"I thought so. My friend was half Cherokee. I guess that's why you remind me of her."

"That might do it."

"Oh, I do have another question. When we saw you at the lake, my friend told me that they call you 'The Noodle Princess'."

She laughed but then said, "I'm no princess. And I would rather you call me Jessie. That's what my friends call me."

"Sure, Jessie. But is it true you 'noodle' for catfish?"

"That would be true."

"How did you get into that?"

"My dad. I grew up tagging along with him. He liked to hunt and fish, and he taught me to noodle. Have you ever been noodling?"

"Nah. I grew up in North Carolina, so I don't know anything about it." He didn't mention his dislike for snakes, after all the venomous ones he encountered in Viet Nam. Vipers, poisonous sea snakes, he didn't trust them.

"You should try it sometime."

"Maybe.... Anyway, I just wanted to meet you. Have fun tonight, Jessie."

"You, too! See ya'!"

Jessie turned to head back into the crowd, just as Carly Jane picked up the mike to sing. Joshua was not expecting her to launch into Stevie Nicks' "Edge of Seventeen," but she did, and she did a nice job. As she sang, Joshua spotted Paul Scarborough, of all people, off to the side talking to someone. When that someone turned, Joshua noted that he was the same guy who led the "Hotty Toddy" cheer back at the bar. This time, he wore hunting gear instead of school-boy, preppy clothes.

What was clear was that the two of them were having a heated argument. Paul jabbed his finger into the guy's chest, until that guy grabbed his hand. A big burly guy, who looked like a combination Green Beret and night club bouncer, leaned in to intervene, but preppy man waved him off. Sensing that he was about to be on the losing end of the stick, Paul got in one final verbal jab and retreated.

"That was really strange," Joshua muttered. "What was that all about?"

The crowd roared as Carly Jane finished her song, and she hopped off stage to fetch a beer. Intercepting her, Joshua asked, "Hey, nice job. You sing well!"

"Well, I try to," she said. "I love it."

"Got a question. You see that guy standing over there, next to the big boy who looks like a bouncer?"

"Yeah?"

"What's his name?"

"Man, you're not from around here, are you?" she quipped. "That's Bubba Bryce. Everybody knows him. This is his farm. Check that - his plantation. All this and more. He owns farmland on both sides of the river. Several thousand acres."

"So, he's the host, then? Tell me about him."

"I don't know a lot. He's a third, I think. Silver spoon-type, a son of planters. His granddaddy was William Bennett Bryce - Mr. Will - and his daddy was a junior - Mr. Bill. They called this one Bubba, 'cause the other names were taken, I guess."

"Tell me more."

"Well, let's see. He went to Ole Miss, then law school, and then he became this big-time lawyer down in Jackson. But, his daddy died suddenly of a heart attack, so he came back home to look after the farm."

"If he owns this much prime farmland, he must be pretty well-off."

"I'll say. He has his own plane and airstrip, plus a nice boat and his own cabin and dock on the river. He likes to party - a lot. And the best thing is, he really knows how to party."

"What do you mean?"

"Well, let's just say he keeps his friends supplied."

"Are you talking about what I think you are talking about?"

"Yep. He doesn't sell it, but he grows it for partying."

"How does he get away with that?"

"Seriously? Who do you think helped get the Sheriff

elected, and the mayor, for that matter?"

"Ah.... And he was a lawyer?"

"Yeah, still is, but don't let that fool ya'. All kinds of things go on in the Delta, legal or not. The Delta is a big, wide-open place."

"Guess so," Joshua said, but he wondered why Bryce would be arguing with Paul.

"I don't know. He's a good dude. He even loans folks money when they need it," she continued. Alarm bells began to go off in Joshua's mind. "Yeah, he loaned us the money for our new PA system and equipment."

"That's nice," he said and wondered if he ever loaned Paul any money to cover his gambling debts. "So, were ya'll able to pay him back?"

"Oh yeah! Bubba might be nice to us, but he's not someone you want to mess with, either."

"I will take that under advisement."

The band was getting ready to start up again, and Carly Jane wandered off in search of her next beer or whatever. Joshua thought about what he had learned. It was hard to focus on the party with all the new information buzzing around in his brain. What if Paul owed Bryce money? Would Bryce take out Dee Dee if Paul didn't pay up? Surely not! But did Paul think so? Was that why they were arguing?

The sound of someone yelling interrupted his reverie. He looked up to see Carly Jane screaming at one of equipment managers for the band, and he was giving it right back. Hands waving, faces red, they were getting after it. Was it about to get physical? The whole crowd began to press in to watch the confrontation. Then, Mr. Green Beret Bouncer Boy waded into the fray, and the crowd parted for him like the Red Sea parted for Moses. He snatched her up like she was a cheap mannequin and put her in a restraint hold. He glared at the manager, who wilted and then faded into the crowd. That was when Bubba Bryce showed up.

"Dadgum it, Carly Jane! Can't you behave? If you can't act

right, you can leave. This is my place and my party, and I'm not having it, ya' hear?"

She stared back defiantly, but then her anger began to fade. The big guy gently set her down onto her feet, just as her husband emerged from the crowd. He took her by the hand and led her away, tears streaking down her cheeks. With the fight over, the party buzz resumed. Mr. GBBB wandered off, and Bubba Bryce went back to working the crowd and revving up the party.

Joshua figured that it was probably time for him to go.

***

As he drove back to town, he realized he was not ready to cash it in. In fact, he was burning to tell Darnell what he had learned. He parked out in front of Miss Flo and Mr. Frankie's place and headed inside.

"Hello!" he called out to the empty diner.

With a cough, Miss Flo rounded the corner from the kitchen and answered, "Come on in, Joshua! You hungry? Want a burger?"

"Not tonight, thanks. I was wondering if I could talk to Darnell."

"Sure. FRANKIE!"

"WHAT?!"

"Go get Darnell for Joshua!" Within a few moments, he emerged from the kitchen. "What's up?"

"Hey. Can we talk for a bit?"

"Sure. I think Auntie Flo and Uncle Frankie are about to close up, so let's go back to my room."

"You mean I finally get to see the mystery apartment?"

"Yeah, here you go," Darnell said, holding the door open for them.

"Very nice, very nice!" Joshua said, taking in the eggshell white walls, the high ceiling with recessed lighting, the colorful rugs scattered about the wood-paneled floor, and the plush leather sofa and lounger. Two lamps were glowing on matching end tables, and Coltrane was playing softly on the stereo. There were paintings on the wall and twin bookshelves were filled.

"Have a seat. What's going on?"

"I just got back from a big party."

"Good for you! Have fun?"

"I guess, but I found out some things I thought you might need to know."

"OK. Where was the party?"

"It was at Bubba Bryce's place."

"Well, well, well! Lucky you! How did you rate an invitation to the Big Man's party?"

"Actually, I didn't. A person with the band invited me as their guest, so I went."

"How were the deer ribs? I've heard they are great, but guys like me don't get invited to his parties, so I've never tasted them."

"Because you're a cop?"

Darnell stared at him meaningfully for a beat and then said, "So, what did you want to tell me?"

"Well, while I was there, I saw Bryce with Paul Scarborough. They were having a big argument. Paul was yelling and poking the guy in the chest. So, I was curious and asked someone about this guy, which was when I found out who he is. That someone also told me that Bryce grows that 'funny tobacco' to supply his pals.... for the party." Darnell looked unimpressed and shrugged his shoulders. "Here's the deal: he is so well off that he loans people money."

"OK, but where are you heading with this?"

"Paul likes to gamble and does it a lot. How does he afford it? Is it possible that Bryce bankrolled him? Were they fighting over money at the party tonight? And if this guy grows marijuana, I'm thinking he's not exactly a law-abiding citizen. What if he had Dee Dee killed because Paul would not pay up? Maybe that's what he and Paul were fighting over."

"Whoa, whoa, whoa! Hold your horses, cowboy! Bubba Bryce is one of the wealthiest and most powerful men in the Delta. You can't just make those kinds of allegations without substantial evidence. You can't afford to speculate with men like him."

"I get that, but don't you think it's a lead worth pursuing?"

"Maybe, but here's the problem. First, he's not in my jurisdiction. He lives in the county, so he is under the Sheriff's jurisdiction. Second, it's a big leap from growing 'wacky weed' on the side to hiring hit men. I will say, however, that he has been known to defend some big-time dealers in the past," Darnell said, scratching his chin.

"See!" Joshua leapt in.

"We would need more evidence, and you can't get that kind of evidence without leverage over someone or a subpoena. We don't have anything that would entice any judge in his right mind to grant a subpoena."

"There might be another way," Joshua began. "What if you have an eyewitness to some hanky-panky? Would that create enough leverage to get someone to talk?"

"If, and I mean if, there's something to find, who's going to be that witness?"

"Do you remember what I did in 'Nam?"

"Uh, you said you were in intelligence?"

"Yes, and I made many a trip to the back country to gather intel."

"This is not a good idea. You are talking trespassing here! And surely he has folks working for him all over that farm you would have to get past. And those old boys are gonna' have shotguns. Remember that song by Hank, Jr.? 'A Country Boy Can Survive.' And if you got caught, I'm telling you, this is not a guy you want to make your enemy."

"Well, then, I just won't get caught."

Darnell did not look convinced. "This is not a good idea," he repeated. "You're jumping to way too many conclusions! Slow down! Don't do anything stupid! I still don't get why you're so obsessed with this, anyway."

CHAPTER FOURTEEN
In Country

Sunday was his regular day off, and after a late night at the party and hanging with Darnell, Joshua was looking forward to sleeping in. Thus, the early morning tapping on his living room door came as a surprise. His mouth felt like he was chewing cotton, his vision was blurry, and his brain was fuzzy, so he wound up stumbling down the stairs to open the door in his normal sleeping attire - his boxers. There stood Miss Flo, her mouth forming a giant "O."

"Oh, Miss Flo, I'm so sorry," he said, hiding himself behind the door. With only his head sticking out, he said, "What can I do for you?"

"Oh, sugar, I'm sorry. I should have known how tired you'd be after a late night."

"Don't worry about it."

"I was just checking to see if you might like to go to church with us," she said wistfully. "It would do you good. Like we sing, 'I'm gonna' lay down my burdens, down by the riverside."

"Uh, well, uh, I'm pretty bushed after last night. Can I get a rain check?"

"Is that a promise?" she asked with a big grin.

"Sure," he muttered.

"OK, then. See you later."

"Sure," he repeated as he shut the door.

He stumbled back upstairs to the restroom to relieve himself, and after washing his hands, he fell back into bed. He had been asleep maybe thirty minutes before there was another knock at the door. This time it was the kitchen door leading to the gravel parking lot. Mumbling curses under his breath, he descended to the door, but this time he had the presence of mind to put on his bathrobe and smooth down his intense "bedhead." Opening the door, he met a smiling Greg.

"Hey, I was just wondering what you were up to. Checking to see if maybe you wanted to do something today," Greg said.

Joshua knew there was no going back to sleep, so he invited Greg in, flipped on the radio, and proceeded to make a pot of coffee. With a giant mug in one hand and two aspirin in the other, he sat down on his couch and invited Greg to join him. Sipping his coffee thoughtfully, he reflected that he had to work tomorrow night to make up for his Saturday night off, so what should they do today? About that time, the oldies rock station in Jackson played "Green River" by CCR.

"Maybe we should go fishing this afternoon on the river," Joshua said to Greg.

"We could do that," Greg said. "This might be our last warm day for a while, but fishing would be better on the lake where my boats are."

It did not take long for them to retrieve Greg's fishing gear from his house and head out. On the way, they stopped by Larry's Bait Shop to grab some minnows and worms. Because it was also a deli and gas station, they were able to fill the cooler with beer, ice, and sandwiches. Before long, they were headed west toward the Delta National Forest, of which the lake was a part. It turned into a gorgeous, 70-degree, sunny day in late November. Joshua knew that folks up north wouldn't believe this kind of weather right after Thanksgiving.

Once on the lake, they both breathed a sigh of satisfaction as they popped the top on a can of cold beer. They baited their hooks and waited. They caught fish off and on, with Greg keeping the bigger ones in a Styrofoam cooler but throwing the smaller ones back. The crappie seemed plentiful, and they caught a couple of bass. In between catches, they talked of football and life in the Delta. As the sun stood straight up in the sky, they took a break for lunch. The cold cut sandwiches hit the spot.

Although there was no current to speak of on the lake, the

gentle breeze pushed their little bass boat south. Time passed, and they caught fewer and fewer fish. They threw one small catfish back. Joshua remembered the "Noodle Princess" as he did so. They did not mind catching fewer fish, because the cold beer was still going down real good. Before he knew it, Joshua was napping. The only way he knew he was asleep was that he was awakened suddenly by the noise of a single-engine plane taking off nearby. Looking up, he saw a Piper Cadet roar into the sky.

"I didn't know there was an airport near this lake," he said drowsily.

"Well, there's not really. It's just a grass landing strip on that plantation over there," Greg replied.

"Whoever owns that land must be pretty well-to-do."

"Yeah. I think it belongs to some big-time Jackson lawyer. I think his name is Bubba Bryce."

Joshua's ears perked up, and he was wide awake now. When he took those twisting country roads to the Hunting Club party in the dark, he did not realize the lake was this close to Bubba's land. An idea began to form in his mind. An idea for later.

***

Tuesday and work came quickly, too quickly after a busy weekend. Joshua barely had time on Monday to clean his apartment and then go to the laundromat and the grocery store. As he drove for his errands, he ruminated on an idea he was forming. What if he did a little recon, like in the old days in 'Nam? What if he sneaked onto Bubba's land to see what he was really up to? Could he find out enough to get some leverage for Darnell to question him? There had to be a connection between him, Paul Scarborough, and Dee Dee.

In the meantime, to work he went. As he pulled into the alley to park, he was surprised to see Sabrina standing there. In fact, she was standing next to the dumpster, about where he found Dee Dee. She seemed to be staring off into space. However, she jerked into motion when she heard his VW easing into the alley. She quickly threw something into the dumpster. Turning, she walked rapidly into the Boiler Room, obviously trying to act as though she had not seen him.

"What the...?" Joshua said, putting his bus in first, setting the parking brake, and turning off the motor. "That was really strange."

He began to walk towards the back door of the bar, but he stopped short, something tickling at his brain. What was she throwing away? Walking over to the dumpster, he looked inside. It was almost full, so what she threw in was on top. He reached in and retrieved one of the sheets of paper that were spilling into the trash. It was a playbill from *Streetcar.* On the front, in large script, right under the title of the play, were the words, "Featuring Dee Dee Scarborough." Joshua looked up and turned towards the back door.

That's odd, he thought. Not that she was throwing away the playbills; it was the way she was acting as she did. He remembered his maxim; one he learned the hard way in Viet Nam: Under the right circumstances, anyone can become a killer. Had Sabrina simply encountered the right circumstances? Was she a jealous wife turned murderer? Was he working for a killer?

Keeping his thoughts to himself, he trudged into the bar.

"Hey, Joshua! 'Bout time you showed up!" Sabrina greeted him with a smile.

Joshua noted the difference between the way she looked in the alley and the way she was acting now. He decided it was best to let it go, for now, so he greeted her with a smile and jumped into the routine.

The night passed by slowly, until Carly Jane came in. She was always good for some fun. "What'll you have?" he asked. "Wait, let me guess. Since I don't have what you really want, you'll take a Jack and Coke, right?"

"You know me too well!" she said and giggled. He sat her drink on a coaster on the bar and watched her take a sip. The questions were bubbling up inside him.

"Hey, Carly Jane, mind if I ask you a question?" She nodded

yes. He started with an easy one. "What was the fight about at the party?"

She blushed and said, "Yeah, I really showed my butt, didn't I?"

"Meh," Joshua shrugged.

"Well, it was simple. I wanted to do another song, and my husband Jeff - he's the lead singer -said fine. But, the manager - Jimmy - thought the crowd wanted to hear some other stuff. We both had had a little to drink, and one thing led to another. I said something I shouldn't have and, well, you saw the rest," she ended sheepishly.

"Ah, it happens to all of us. I saw something else, too," he said, easing into his next question. "Did you see Bubba and Paul Scarborough fighting? Well, not fighting really, just having words." She shook her head no. "I wonder what that was about?"

"Who knows?" she shrugged.

"So, tell me more about this Bubba Bryce. What does he do besides the lawyer thing, grow funny tobacco, and run the farm?"

"Uh, fix me another one, and I will tell you," she said and laughed. Putting the drink on her coaster, he looked at her questioningly.

"I shouldn't have told you about what he does for his friends. Are you a narc?"

Joshua burst out laughing. "Hardly!" he sputtered. "Just a curious bartender."

"Well, remember what they say about those curious cats," she said straight-faced.

"Yeah, so let's skip that part. What does a rich planter do in his spare time?"

"Well, he does like to fly. Got his own plane and stuff. I hear he likes to vacation on the Gulf Coast. He even flies down to Key West and all."

Joshua's eyes widened, and he turned away to mask his excitement. The Keys. He was thinking that a lot of stuff goes on in the Keys, especially if you are rich and into drugs. And sometimes it's the drugs that make you rich. Or help pay the bills.

"Wow! Must be nice to fly down to the Keys whenever you feel like it," he said. "Ever got the chance to go with him?"

"Nah, but that would be fun. I heard that he is going down this week in fact. Coming back Sunday night."

Ah, here we go! Joshua thought. Wonder what he brings back with him? Joshua had heard stories about "bullet boats" bringing cocaine into the Thousand Islands area just south of the Everglades. Too many islands, too much swampy land, and not enough police presence to stop anything going on there.

"Well, I need to get going," Carly Jane said. "Headed to the Jitney Jungle to pick up some groceries. Shopping is always more fun with a couple of drinks in me," she said and laughed.

Getting information from you is lot easier that way, too, he thought.

***

It took a few days for his plan to take shape. He was grateful he had kept his night vision goggles and 35 mm camera from 'Nam, and even more grateful he had brought them with him when he got his things from North Carolina. The temperature was finally dropping, but Gibson's Discount had black sweatshirts, skull caps, and insulated underwear. They also had black shoe polish to smear on his face for anti-glare. They even had slow speed 35 mm film. Greg Jensen was happy to let Joshua borrow his fishing boat.

The plan was simple. Next Sunday afternoon, he would go fishing on the lake next to Bubba Bryce's farm. When it got dark, he would pull into a little creek and tie up. There, he would change into dark clothing, grease his face, and trek in as close as he could get to Bryce's place. Hopefully, he would see something that he could capture on film. With the slow speed film and correct f-stop and camera speed settings, he should be able to get some decent pictures without a flash. He pictured the look on Darnell's face when he showed them to him. If he got something, anyway.

His day off, Sunday, finally came. As he drove his VW bus down the dirt road beside the lake, the sounds of "Bad Moon Rising" by Creedence Clearwater Revival came on the radio. He remembered the song from his days in 'Nam, and he also remembered what the song was talking about. He hoped there was not a bad moon rising. He seriously hoped not. Not tonight. Nonetheless, John Fogarty sang on. "Don't go around tonight, Well it's bound to take your life, There's a bad moon on the rise."

He got to the lake later in the afternoon and fished a while. As the sun began to set in orange flames, Joshua noticed that the lake was now deserted. It was colder than he expected, as a north wind began to whip across the lake. "Mississippi really does have a winter, after all," he said to the wind.

Stowing his fishing pole, he engaged the electric troll motor and began to look for one of the tiny creeks that flowed into the lake, one that was near where he had seen the plane take off before. Finding one, he was able to get far enough in to be out of sight. He tied up, just as dusk fell. And then he saw the moon rising. He kept telling himself that it was too cold in early December for snakes to be out. Still, he donned the night vision goggles and began to tread carefully through the thick underbrush. The going was easier once he got into the trees.

Slowly and quietly, he stepped closer and closer to what would be Bubba Bryce's property. Eventually, he saw a light in the distance. Time to take off the night vision goggles and use the camera's telephoto lens like binoculars. What he saw was typical of a Delta farm. A barn or shed lit by a security light, like the one in the bar's alley. In the distance, he saw what looked like some old shacks. And then, farther away, something glowing white in the moonlight. Slowly, his eyes adjusted more, and he realized that he was looking at the old antebellum mansion on Bryce's plantation. On the other side of that, in the distance, another security light glowed weakly, and Joshua recognized the Quonset hut-like barn where the Deer Party had been held.

That was when a pickup truck ground to a halt in front of the nearer barn, its deer lights blazing in front of it. A man got out of the truck and went in. He returned with a box, put it in the bed of the truck, and hopped into the cab. He slowly drove nearer, but parallel, to Joshua's position. Suddenly, a burning light flared. The truck drove on, and then another light flared. It took him a second to realize that the driver of the truck was putting out flares along the runway. Soon, Joshua was able to make out the grass landing strip. The man finished with the flares and returned to the barn. Almost simultaneously, Joshua began to hear the drone of a small engine plane. Looking to his right, he saw its landing lights and taillight in the distance. This was it. This is what he had come for. Would Bubba have cargo from the Keys? From South America? Could he capture that on camera?

Slowly the plane descended, and as it did, the truck's lights blinked like Morse Code. Then, the plane touched down and coasted towards the barn and the truck. The plane stopped, and its pilot killed the engine. The man in the pickup rushed forward, and the pilot disembarked. Because of the light from the security pole and the deer lights from the truck, Joshua could see fairly well. Peering through the camera's lens, he realized he was looking at Bubba Bryce and his ex-military, body building, bodyguard. He began to snap pictures quickly.

And then, there it was. The two men began to offload black garbage bags, filled to the brim. Joshua kept taking pictures, even though he could not see what was in the bags. Until, that is, he got very lucky. Bubba pulled something from one of the bags and held it up for the other man to see. Whatever it was, was white, and it was wrapped tightly in plastic. Joshua had just hit pay dirt. He had proof positive, on film, that Bubba was smuggling drugs.

And that was when he ran out of luck. Somehow, his presence or the sound of his camera snapping pictures disturbed some creature nearby. With a god-awful screech, a large bird launched into the air from a tree above him, its massive wings whooshing through the cold night air. Startled, Joshua couldn't suppress a yelp. It was likely an owl, but the two men suddenly stopped. They froze in place and stared directly towards him. He realized two things very quickly. One, they might not have seen him - yet - but they had heard him yelp. Suddenly, both men leapt into the truck and fired it up. In shock, Joshua realized that the truck was racing towards him!

It seemed like an eternity passed before he could shake off the shock, but when he did, he was all arms and legs, scrabbling back into the dense canopy. And none too soon. He heard the bullets snipping through the air above him before he heard the discharge of a weapon. What he heard was the unmistakable bark of an AK-47, which was what the Viet Cong used in 'Nam. The truck ground closer, and the AK began to bark again.

"What the hell was I thinking!" he gasped as he crawled away. That was when it occurred to him. If they had an AK, why wouldn't they protect their property with Claymore mines, some trip-wired and some remote-controlled? No time to worry about that now, much less snakes. His heart pounded as he jumped to his feet and began to run. He became aware that he no longer heard the AK or the truck. Looking back, he saw flashlights bobbing through the trees. They were coming for him! Finally, after what felt like an eternity, he reached the fishing boat and shoved out into the water. He began to head back towards the landing where he could store the boat and leave in his VW.

That was when he heard the truck roar back into life, and it hit him like an electric shock. They must have figured out that whoever they were chasing had come across the lake by boat. And where was the nearest dock? Exactly! Joshua shoved the rudder all the way to the right and did a quick about face, heading away from the dock where his VW was parked. Looking back over his shoulder as he fled, he saw the pickup slide to a stop exactly where he had been heading. In the distance, he could see the men hop out of the truck. Then, one of them grabbed the spotlight. Its light jabbed across the lake like the flicking tongue of a dragon, spitting fire meant to destroy him.

"I have got to find another creek, another inlet to hide in," he muttered.

And then, he got lucky again. He spotted an inlet to a bigger creek. He sped into it as fast as the little electric motor would take him. Fortunately, the creek's source was a swamp-like pond, big enough to conceal himself. Joshua steered the boat behind a fallen tree and took refuge behind its mass of Spanish moss. And then, he laid down in the boat. He waited, listening intently for any sound. He jumped as some creature snapped twigs and bounded into the night. Once it was gone, he heard bats chittering in the darkness overhead. No droning cicadas tonight or singing frogs for that matter. It was too cold. Even with his sweatshirt and insulated underwear, Joshua could not stop shivering. There was as yet no sound of an approaching truck, or human for that matter. Still, he waited, trying to slow his breathing. Like the Apostle Paul and his companions in the biblical shipwreck, he found himself "praying for daylight."

***

Joshua did not know when he nodded off. He was surprised that his fear and the cold let him sleep. He woke with a start, remembering where he was and what had happened. He also recognized that he was cold, really cold. Peering carefully over the side of the boat, he saw that dawn was approaching. The sun was not yet quite up, but what he could see looked like a primeval swamp. Giant cypress trees, dripping Spanish moss, dotted the murky brown waters of the swamp, and a wet, chilly fog hung in the air. If a T-Rex had come crashing through the trees, Joshua would not have been surprised.

Still. That was the word of the day. Still. All was still, and all was quiet. Had the danger passed? There was only one way to find out. Joshua fired up the trolling motor and began to putter towards the creek that led to the lake. Before long, the sun was up. As he continued up the lake towards the dock, he heard nothing and saw nothing. Until, that is, he saw his trusty VW bus beside the dock. He sighed in relief. And that's when it dawned on him. They had been there the night before. At the dock. And they, too, had seen his VW. How many baby blue VW's with a white top were there in Indian Springs?

"What the hell was I thinking?!"

Indeed.

CHAPTER FIFTEEN
Back in the World

The old expression, "caught between a rock and a hard place," came to mind. Joshua was shivering in the boat. Getting to shore under some outstretched branches, out of the wind, helped some, but the sun was still low in the sky. He was also really, really hungry. He had not thought to bring food or water. He had not thought: that was the gist of it. Should he return to his VW and hightail it home? What if Bubba and beefed-up GI Joe were watching the road? He had to decide and soon. He couldn't sit in this boat all day.

Slowly, a plan began to develop in his mind. There was more than one dock on this lake, even as small as it was. Likely six or seven. Some of the docks had small cabins or RV's where the fishermen could stay overnight. In fact, Greg had a small cabin next to his dock. It was possible that Bubba and Joe might deduce that his VW belonged merely to a fisherman camping overnight. They could not definitively conclude that was where the trespasser came from. Maybe. Still, Joshua did not want to encounter them in his VW on the way out. That could get ugly.

"I've got to do something!" he blurted. The cold and hunger made it hard to think straight. And then, he remembered that there was a store farther down the lake. It took some time and some trial and error, but eventually he found the dock nearest the bait shop. He secured the boat to a cleat on the small dock with Greg's chain and padlock. At least he thought of that. Still shaking from the cold, he began to walk to the store. Fortunately, no one seemed to be around. After all, it wasn't exactly peak season for fishing or boating. Nonetheless, the store was open. Like a lot of small stores in the Delta, this one was the owner's life. His customers were his friends. Joshua needed something to eat, and he needed to get warm. The store had both. He was able to buy a cup of coffee and a Honey Bun. And, for a few minutes, he got warm while he ate. The storekeeper asked no questions; he simply continued to stock his shelves. Joshua figured that was for the best.

He finished his coffee and another Honey Bun. As he ate, he decided what to do. In his mind, Bubba and his goon could prove nothing. So what if he saw them on the way out? He was just another fisherman. He thanked the storekeeper and returned to the boat. Before long, he was tying up at Greg's dock. He also put the troll motor battery on the charger for him. That was the least he could do. His trusty VW fired up first thing, and Joshua was on his way.

And then, there they were. Bubba Bryce and his henchman, waiting beside the road in the pickup truck with the deer lights. He didn't have time to turn away. Instinctively, he gave the noncommittal, Southern head nod to say "Hide-ee." They nodded back, and that was it. They did not follow. Joshua drove on, breathing a sigh of relief, congratulating himself on making his escape. All's well that ends well, he thought.

Still, doubt nagged at the back of his mind. They knew his VW now, and they knew he was on the lake the night before. And the intrusion on their land and their illegal business? They wouldn't just let that go. Joshua tried to tell himself that he was not afraid of them, but regardless, he wasn't stupid. They had already shown that they were willing to shoot to kill, like any other drug dealers. The only reason they didn't have barbed wire and Claymore mines, he figured, was because they were so far out in the sticks. He kept reminding himself that they couldn't prove anything. If they ever confronted him, he could tell them that he was fishing and slept over in the cabin, like several other people on the lake. But what if they had banged on that cabin door, with no response? What then? Joshua decided he could tell them some lie. He could say that he was a light sleeper, so he always slept with ear plugs. That's why he didn't hear them knocking. Still, he was on their radar, and that was not a comfortable thought.

When he made it home, he took a shower and then devoured a large, country breakfast. Afterward, he went straight to bed.

***

Sleep did not come easily. He tossed and turned as strange images from the night before flashed disjointedly through his mind. The muzzle flash of the AK-47, the black bags, the flares, the plane. Sleep finally came, but it brought with it vivid dreams. Joshua found himself back in the jungle, the leaves dripping from a recent rain, his shirt sticking to his skin. The heat was consuming, and the smells of jungle decay surrounded him. Then, he heard someone softly muttering in Vietnamese. Viet Cong! He ducked behind a tree. Then, there came the sound of helicopters, their blades beating the air in the darkness. A brilliant flash followed, and a jet thundered overhead before he heard the concussion of the napalm bomb. The heat and pressure washed past him, and he heard inhuman cries in the distance. AK-47's and M-16's thudded nearby. Joshua could smell cordite and burning flesh, mixed with the stench of fear. And then, he saw her. It was Addie, running through the trees. In a panic, he leaped forward and raced after her. His heart pounded in his chest as he called out to her. Vainly he tried to catch her, but soon he lost her in the dense foliage. He screamed in anguish and frustration.

He woke up, covered in sweat. The sheets were in disarray, just like his mind.

***

On Tuesday morning, Joshua's next dilemma was getting the hard-fought-for film developed. He could simply take it to the drug store, but there was the issue of the guy down there paying too much attention to what was being developed. He would likely recognize Bubba, and it wouldn't take an expert to figure out what they were doing. He could turn the film over to Darnell and let the police deal with it. Joshua didn't like that option, either. If Bubba had the local Sheriff in his pocket, might he also not have someone in the police department? The film might just "disappear," or the news of it might just make it to Bubba, who could clean up his place temporarily. And dispose of Joshua, for that matter. At any rate, he would rather have multiple copies of the pictures, for safekeeping.

His decision was therefore easy, or so he thought. He would develop the film himself. He had done so before in 'Nam, so he could do it here. The problem would not be a dark room - he could use his bathroom for that, nor would the problem be the chemicals and the trays - he could buy that. The problem would be the printer. Using his phone book, Jonah could not find a photo / hobby shop for the chemicals, however. Not only was there nothing in Indian Springs, but there wasn't anything nearby, either. So much for that idea. And then he remembered. One of the regulars at the bar was the editor of the *Indian Springs Reporter.* Maybe he could ask that guy to let him use his equipment. He would need a printer anyway. But what story would he use to get the editor to agree? How about the promise of first dibs on the big story, when the story of Bubba's arrest and relationship to the murder of Dee Dee hit the streets? That would sell. On the other hand, letting a reporter know about things like that now could be a problem. Better not to have them sniffing around.

And that was when the enormity of what happened hit him. Maybe he had been in shock, but the weight of his near-death experience finally landed on him. What the heck was he doing? What was he trying to prove? He risked his life for a shaky theory about Bubba and his connection to Paul and the murder of Dee Dee. His goal all along was to get something on Bubba, so they could leverage that for information on Paul Scarborough. If it got a hard-core drug dealer off the streets, more the merrier. That was when he realized that he was not quite the intelligence officer he used to be, or thought he was, for that matter. He had survived his encounter with Bubba Bryce not from skill but from sheer luck and the enormous wilderness that was the Delta National Forest. He came way too close to being just another statistic.

Why was he so obsessed with finding Dee Dee's killer, anyway? And then it hit him. Addie. This was all about Addie. He could not solve her mystery, so he was trying to solve this one. What do psychiatrists call such behavior? Transference? Or was it compensation? Was he trying to make up for something? His guilt in the matter? Was it worth dying for? Maybe it was time to put this amateur sleuth business on the shelf for a bit. Let things cool down a little, especially with Bubba Bryce. So, Joshua wound the roll of film in his camera, took it out, and placed it in a film canister. He placed the canister on the bookshelf, behind his copy of Churchill's biography. It should be safe there.

***

Tuesday afternoon, he drove down to the bar for work. Hanging his jacket on the community coat rack, he saw Sabrina sitting at one of the tables. Her eyes seemed distant, unfocused. As he approached, he saw a box of Christmas decorations sitting in front of her.

"Hey, Sabrina, you decorating for Christmas?" he asked.

Sabrina sighed deeply and looked up at him. "Not much in the mood for it."

"Isn't Christmas supposed to be 'the most wonderful time of the year?'" he said and smirked.

Sabrina responded by tossing a Christmas ornament back into the box. "Joshua, I'm just tired. Tired of this place. Tired of being a suspect in a murder."

"Come on, Sabrina. Things have quieted down on that front. It's been almost six months."

"Yeah, well, what you might not know is that word is on the street about me. My buddies in the PD kept it quiet for a long time, but this is a small town, and everybody talks," she said with a huff. "People look at me funny at the grocery store. When they see me coming, they suddenly clam up and turn away."

"That's got to be tough."

"Yes," Sabrina agreed. "And what you might not know is that all this time, your *buddy* Darnell just so happens to run into me, no matter where I go. He's even dropped by here a few times to ask more questions."

Joshua recognized the tried-and-true police method: keep the pressure on a suspect until they break. Comes in handy when you have no real evidence. He said, "I don't know what to say. I'm sorry. I wish they could find out something more and solve this case."

"You and me both! Well, these decorations won't put themselves up, although I wish they would! Thanks for listening."

Sabrina shuffled off to string up some lights, leaving Joshua in her dismal wake. Christmas was not his favorite time of the year, either. He knew why he felt that way, but he also knew he had it in his power to do something to help Sabrina. He decided that he needed to talk to Darnell, regardless of the consequences.

The evening passed quickly, and then Scott burst in from the theater. He bussed his bride's cheek and then headed to the bar. He did not seem to notice the sour look on Sabrina's face. Joshua grabbed a Coors Light from the cooler, popped the top, and set it gingerly on a bar napkin.

"So, how is Sabrina holding up?"

"I don't know, man. This crap is wearing her down."

"I can't imagine. She might need a hug right now, in fact," he said, nodding toward Sabrina.

***

"What the hell were you thinking?"

Such was Darnell's reaction when Joshua told him about his recent recon mission at Bubba Bryce's place. His eyes were wide, and the veins in his neck popped out. "You could have been killed! That was so stupid. And for what? Some half-baked theory about Dee Dee's death? You are messing with the wrong people. Bubba carries a lot of weight in these parts, and he has a lot of friends."

Suddenly, Joshua's cheeseburger didn't taste so good anymore. "Yeah, well, when I heard that AK go off, I knew I had messed up."

"You were damn lucky! Are you sure they didn't ID you?"

"You are right of course, but no, they never saw me. And I did get some good pictures."

"Of what?"

"Bubba and his grunt unloading bags of white powder. Cocaine maybe? Heroin? Or something else?"

The detective's eyes focused intently on Joshua. "And this is gonna' solve Dee Dee's murder how?"

"Like I said, if the Mississippi Bureau of Investigation were to take Bubba down, they could squeeze him for some information. I'm telling you, Bubba and Paul Scarborough are connected. I saw them at the deer party, and they were having a major disagreement."

"Paul is not the only suspect, Joshua."

"I know, but he is the most likely one, in my mind."

Darnell huffed. "So, what do you want me to do?"

"I want to give you the film. Get it developed. Just not here. If Bubba has friends in the Sheriff's office, he probably has some in the police department."

"I guess I could give it to the MBI. Bubba is not in my jurisdiction anyway."

"I want you to see the pictures for yourself, and I want to see them, also. Call me paranoid, but after what I went through, I want a set for myself just in case. Don't you have some friends in another police department that could develop and print them? We could pass a set and the intel along to the MBI."

"I suppose, but here's what I want to know. Why does this mean so much to you? I didn't know you were so anti-drug. You had to have seen a lot of that in 'Nam. Why does solving Dee Dee's murder mean so much to you?"

"OK, the first question is easy to answer. I tried grass a couple of times in 'Nam with the guys, like a lot of other folks. In the long run, though, it just seemed like a waste of time, money, and brain cells to me. Plus, it was illegal. So, I didn't really make a habit of it. If Bubba were only growing it to party with his friends like I've been told, I wouldn't care about that. But this is different. He is bringing hard-core drugs into this community. You and I both have seen what that does to people and to their families."

"OK, I buy that, but still, why Dee Dee's murder? You barely knew her."

Joshua averted his eyes and said, "Well, my friend Sabrina is still under suspicion, and she is really getting down about it. I feel for her."

"So, you feel for Sabrina, and you're willing to risk your life for her?'

"Maybe I was just too stupid to realize that could happen."

Darnell looked at him for a long minute, wondering what else was going on. "OK. I'll get them developed by some friends down in Jackson. I will give you a set and pass another set along to the MBI, IF, and I mean IF, they show what you think they do."

"Fair enough," Joshua said. He passed the film canister to Darnell and swallowed the last of his beer and burger.

CHAPTER SIXTEEN
"The Most Wonderful Time of the Year"

It was finally, fully cold. Winter had come at last to the Delta. The Boiler Room was completely decorated for Christmas: a large, living fir tree filled with colorful ornaments; lights strung all around; and mistletoe hanging from the rafters. Christmas music was playing on the juke box. That was bad enough for Joshua, but then Sabrina made it worse. The annual Christmas Party, she said. Here at the pub. The bar would be closed for Christmas Eve on Friday, Christmas Day on Saturday, and as usual on Sunday. A three-day weekend! So, Christmas Eve party, 2-5 pm! Close friends and friends of the theater. Christmas Cheer! Woo hoo!

Joshua did not like Christmas. Nothing good ever happened on that day. When Santa Claus showed up at his rusty, single wide on the hill, it must have been his last stop, cause he was usually almost out of presents. No matter how hard his widowed mother worked at the diner, there was very little money for extra's. And that wasn't the worst thing that happened on Christmas. Still, Joshua was EXPECTED to be at the party and help. As good as Sabrina and Scott had been to him, he couldn't say no.

On the Wednesday night before the party, Joshua was pouring beer for a few regulars. The door banged open, and in walked Bubba Bryce and his muscle-headed protection. Joshua looked away quickly, swallowing the lump in his throat. As the two men bellied up to the bar, Joshua looked across the room, hoping that Sabrina could wait on them. Unfortunately, she was gabbing away with some folks at the pool tables.

"What'll you have?" he asked.

"Bud Light in the bottle," Bryce answered.

"Ditto," said GI Woe. "Oh, and can we get some fried dill pickles?"

"Sure," Joshua said, as he pulled two beers out of the cooler, snapped open the caps, and placed them on the bar.

"Thanks," Bubba said, taking a long swig of the beer. Then, "Ah, I think we'll sit at a table over there."

"No problem. I'll bring you the pickles when they come up."

As they went to their seat, Joshua strode through the door to Le Monde to place the order. Returning to the bar, he saw that Bubba was looking at him quizzically. This did not please Joshua, so he ducked down to fiddle with the set-ups under the bar. After a few minutes, their order came up, and he took it to their table. As he was about to turn away, Bubba spoke up.

"Bartender, do I know you? I think I've seen you somewhere before."

Joshua's heart began to beat faster as he stuttered, "I don't think so." Then, as an afterthought, he said, "You've probably just seen me in here."

"No, no, I think I've seen you somewhere before."

Joshua saw an opening. "I think I know where you've seen me. You're the guy who throws that great Hunting Club party. I was there this year."

"Humph," Bubba replied. "Maybe so, but I don't remember inviting you."

Joshua flushed. "Actually, you didn't. Sorry about that. I came as a guest of the band. Hope you don't mind."

"Oh, let me guess. Carly Jane invited you. That girl is a piece of work."

Seeking to move on, Joshua grinned and said, "Can I get ya'll anything else?"

"Nah, we're good. Only got time for one beer."

Joshua breathed a sigh of relief as he headed back to the bar. Still, he could feel Bryce's eyes boring into his back. He tried to reassure himself that there was no way they could have recognized him in the dark that night at the lake. His head was covered with a skull cap, and his face was greased up. The only time they could have seen him otherwise was the next morning when he passed them on the road. Would they eventually put two and two together? Even so, that proved nothing. Before long, they settled up and moved on. Still, Bryce glanced back at Joshua as he headed to the door. When they were gone, Joshua worked at slowing his breathing.

He flinched as Sabrina blurted behind him, "What's up with you? You look like you've seen a ghost."

"Not this time," he sighed.

The jukebox came to life, and the sounds of "A Country Boy Can Survive" by Hank, Jr. filled the bar. As Hank sang about "them ole boys raised up on shotguns," Joshua reflected that Bubba and his boy had more than shotguns. Way more.

***

The afternoon of the Christmas party came around, and Joshua was miserable. He had to work hard on his fake smile as he served beer, wine, and whiskey, reminding himself that he owed it to Sabrina and Scott to help. The bar was certainly lively enough, filled with joyous friends who were overflowing with Christmas cheer. Carly Jane and the Mindbenders were there, as were Rueben and Jeff and Greg and Shelley and many other theater regulars. Detective Darnell Dupont was NOT invited. Dressed in ugly Christmas sweaters, the theme of the party, guests were laughing and joking loudly. Then, "Blue Christmas" by Elvis began to bellow from the juke box. Joshua thought, Of course! Slow dancers edged to the dance floor, the single ones angling to get under the mistle toe.

Carly Jane bounced up to the bar, giggling with excitement, looking for her usual. "What's wrong with you," she asked Joshua. "You look like someone just shot your puppy."

Joshua could not fake a smile for that one. "I don't have a puppy." He turned away. With a puzzled look on her face, Carly Jane left to rejoin the boys in the band.

"Alright, cowboy, you are going to have to lighten up," Sabrina said to Joshua, coming up beside him. He looked at

Sabrina but said nothing. Sabrina grabbed his hand, and before he knew what hit him, she had dragged him through the opening into the restaurant. "What's going on with you!"

"Nothing," he mumbled.

"Yes, there is! You've been moping around here all afternoon. Lighten up! Tomorrow is Christmas!"

"I'm fine," he lied.

"No, you're not, and I'm tired of your tough guy approach!"

"What are you talking about?" he said, knowing exactly what she was talking about.

"Let me spell it out for you. You show up in Indian Springs like a Sad Sack with a broken-down VW. But it was clear from the beginning that there was more going on than just that. It was like you always had to try too hard to enjoy our outings. And that ring on your finger? What's up with that? And this mystery woman you keep alluding to but never want to talk about. What's your story, Mister?"

"Sabrina, I can't. It's just too hard to talk about it."

"Well, suck it up. You were tough enough to be in the Army. Out with it."

Of course, someone would have to play "Forever Yours" by Journey, he thought. As it played, his eyes lost their focus, as his mind drifted back to what had happened.

CHAPTER SEVENTEEN
Christmas Day, 1980

Joshua lounged on the couch, his legs stretched out. Addie was snuggled beside him, her head resting on his chest. Sipping his hot chocolate, he sighed with contentment. Last night, Christmas Eve, they had gone to a Candlelight Communion service at Addie's parents' church. And now, this morning, the twinkling lights of the Christmas tree, the wrapping paper scattered everywhere, the fire in the fireplace crackling and popping, and the snow-covered trees seen through the living room window made this a Norman Rockwell Christmas print. The local radio station playing "White Christmas" by Bing Crosby completed the perfect scene.

Addie turned her head to Joshua and smiled. Oh, that smile! It lit up his world! Then, she leaned in to kiss him. He once again sighed.

He wondered what he did to deserve this kind of happiness. Meeting Addie in his first year as a teacher in '77, getting engaged in the spring of '79, married that same year in the fall. Finding the cute bungalow on the hillside for rent. As teachers, they did not have much, but they were so happy together. Addie made him whole, helping him forget that single-wide on the hill, Viet Nam, and the death of his mother who worked so hard to raise him after his father died. This might just be the first Christmas I've ever really enjoyed, he reflected.

Smiling up at him again, Addie whispered, "I have a secret."

"I thought we promised to never keep secrets from one another!"

"This is a good secret, and I won't be able to keep it much longer."

He looked intently into Addie's dancing eyes and said, "Well, what is it?"

"Do you prefer blue or pink?" she asked coyly.

"What?!"

"Would you like to have a boy or a girl?"

Slowly, he began to understand Addie's secret.

"What? Are you pregnant, Addie?"

"Yes," she beamed, "and I am so happy!"

Joshua frowned. "How did that happen?"

"What do you think, silly?"

Thinking about his impoverished childhood, he blurted, "But we don't make enough money to raise a child!"

Addie's face registered surprise. "You said you wanted children!"

"I do, but I don't know if we're ready," he said. "Can we afford it? I grew up with nothing, and I don't want my child to have to live like that."

"We'll be fine," Addie said tersely.

"You've taken me by surprise. I need time to think about this."

"Well, ready or not, I'm pregnant, and I want this baby!"

"So, I don't have any say in this?"

"Oh, Joshua! I thought you would be so happy! I thought this would be the best day of our lives!" With tears springing to her eyes, she blurted, "I need some space!" She jumped up from the couch; grabbed her purse, car keys, and coat; and stormed out of the front door.

Stunned, Joshua stood up. That sinking feeling in his stomach told him that he had blown it. He had handled it all wrong. Stupid! He raced to the door as Addie fired up her car and spun out of their drive.

"Addie! Stop! I'm sorry! Please stop!" he yelled, chasing the car down the drive, before losing the battle.

"Stupid, stupid, stupid!" He pounded his thigh with his fist as he trudged back to the house. Addie is the love of my life, he reflected. Of course I want children with her! How could I have been so dumb! My mom and I never had much, but we were a family. And Addie and I are both working. Of course, we could make it work. "Just because I was surprised doesn't mean I had to act so stupid!" he snapped, slamming the door behind him.

For him, Christmas was over. Forever.

CHAPTER EIGHTEEN
"Hard Candy Christmas"

"That was the last time I ever saw her," Joshua said and sighed, swiping at his eyes as he turned his head away.

"Oh, Joshua! I'm so sorry! So, ya'll split up?" Joshua shook his head no. "Wait. What happened?"

"That was the last time I ever saw her."

"She disappeared?"

"Yes. When she did not come home by dark, I got worried. I called her parents, and they had not seen her. I called her friends, and they had not seen her, either. Later that night, I drove around looking for her. I went everywhere I could think of, but no dice. At first, I thought she was just mad at me and was staying somewhere away from me. I kept hoping and praying that was the case, that she would come home in the morning, and I could make it right with her."

"But she didn't." Again, Joshua shook his head no. "What did you do?"

"After a sleepless night, I called the local hospital to see if they had seen her. Nope. So then, I called the police, the Sheriff, and the State Troopers. I got her family and friends, and we began to search frantically. But those North Carolina mountains, people don't realize how much territory there is, how much ground there is to cover."

"Joshua, oh God!"

"We prayed. The church prayed. We had a candlelight vigil for her. We even put word out on the news media. We had posters of her on every street corner. Nothing."

"I remember seeing something on TV about a teacher missing in North Carolina. Oh, Joshua, I can't imagine the horror!"

"It was worse than anyone could imagine. I was numb. In a fog. And I felt like it was all my fault. If I hadn't been so stupid, she wouldn't have taken off. And I should have gone after her! I couldn't focus. I tried to go back to work, but I found my mind wandering in the middle of a lecture. We searched and searched for months. And then, one day, the police knocked on my door. They said that they had exhausted all their resources. They would have to call off the search. They told me that I would have to accept the fact that she was gone. I will never forget what they said next. They said that since she had been gone so long without contacting anyone, I needed to accept the fact that she was likely dead, either from an accident or foul play."

"Oh, Joshua, no!"

"You can't imagine all the scenarios that went through my mind. Did her car slide off the road in the snow, down into a gully so deep she could not be seen? Did she die alone, cold and frightened? Knowing that our baby would die with her?" Tears came to Sabrina's eyes, and she just shook her head. "Even worse was the notion that maybe someone snatched her, and... and...."

He could not go on. Sabrina grabbed him and hugged him tight.

After a moment, he broke from the intense hug and said, "Not knowing if she was dead or alive. Knowing that it was my fault, it was hard. I tried so hard to keep it together. I did OK through the summer, but when school started, and they decided to hold a memorial for her, I fell apart. I started drinking. Coming to work late, then calling in sick, then coming in hungover. Then it became no-call, no-show, until one day, not long after Christmas, I showed up drunk at school."

"Joshua." Sabrina sighed.

"The principal called me in, and I thought he was going to fire me. Instead, Addie's mother and father were sitting in his office with him. They told me, 'You are dishonoring the memory of our daughter... and your wife.' I was stunned. Devastated. But then I decided to dedicate the rest of the school year to being my best for her. Still, teaching wasn't the same without her there, doing joint lessons, and so forth. Wasn't sure if I wanted to do it anymore. And that next Christmas! God! After that, the sight of the school, the mountains, without her, just hurt too much. That empty house. Another teacher in her classroom. So, at the end of the year, I decided to travel, to decompress, and take a road trip."

"And then you came here, right?" Sabrina said. Joshua nodded yes. "Oh, my goodness! That's why the sight of 'Noodle Girl' freaked you out. She looked like her. You must have felt like you were seeing a ghost!"

"That was not the only time," he said, remembering Dee Dee lying dead in the parking lot. "I can't tell you what it's like, not knowing whatever became of her. Knowing I could not save her yet hoping that she might turn up. Knowing that she might be out there somewhere."

"I can't imagine." Sabrina paused, then said, "Now I know why you still wear your wedding ring. And that's why you are never interested in another woman or anything." Then, her face lit up with understanding. "Let me guess. She called you 'Josh,' right? That's why you go by Joshua." Joshua nodded yes. Then another thought struck her. "Did the police ever suspect you?"

"I don't think so, not really. I mean, they followed their procedures. They questioned me and all, and they checked out my whereabouts and stuff. They looked through the house, and it still looked like Christmas morning with wrapping paper everywhere. I guess you could say there was no evidence of foul play. Her car was gone, but so was her purse and keys. Plus, everyone knew how crazy we were about each other. Our friends and family used to make fun of how we always held hands and hugged and stuff. They kidded us about it and called us the 'love birds.' In the end, and this is hard to say, but there was no... body.... No evidence of a murder or anything. It looked like she just ran off."

"Joshua, I am so sorry Scott and I insisted you work this party. If we had known...."

"You didn't, so don't worry about it."

"Go home, Joshua. Take a break, OK?"

"OK. But please keep this between us."

He left through the side door, the sounds of "Have Yourself a Merry Little Christmas" trailing behind him. He fired up his VW and pulled out. Before he knew it, he was parked in the liquor store lot, not really remembering the drive over or the decision to go there.

"A fifth of Jim Beam and a liter of Coke, please," he said to the attendant. He paid up, ignoring the twinkling Christmas lights and the sounds of Michael Jackson's "Santa Claus Is Coming to Town." He hurried out.

He had no sooner parked his VW and entered his apartment, before he heard a knock on his first-floor hallway door. Opening it, he was surprised to see Miss Flo and Mr. Frankie there.

"Hey, Joshua," said Flo in her gravelly voice. "We were just headed out to our Candlelight Communion service at church, and we thought maybe you would like to go."

Joshua groaned inwardly. Tonight of all nights to go to a Christmas Eve service. Memories of his last night with Addie crowded in on him.

"Uh, that was mighty nice of you to think of me," he replied, "but I just got off from working a special party down at the Boiler Room, and I'm really tired."

"This would be a nice opportunity for you to make good on promise to go to church with us," she persisted.

Joshua had forgotten about his promise and was kicking himself for making it. "Some other time, OK. Ya'll enjoy it. And Merry Christmas." He moved to shut the door before they could object, even though doing so made him feel like a jerk.

"Joshua, wait! Flo said. "I can't help but think that tonight, of all nights, you need to go with us. Listen, all of us carry a burden. All of us have baggage. I don't know about you, but I don't want to spend my life like I'm on a never-ending Greyhound bus trip, lugging my baggage from station to station. I want to get home and lay my baggage down."

Joshua shook his head and shut the door. He returned to

the kitchen, where he mixed the first of many whiskeys and Coke.

***

The loud, piercing ring of his telephone jarred Joshua upright. That swift motion sent a pain through his head that felt like an ice pick to the brain. Through his blurry eyes and aching head, he could see that he was sitting on the living room couch, where he had obviously slept. He could also see an empty Jim Beam bottle laying on the floor. The incessant ringing of the phone threatened to split his head open, and he realized that he had the mother of all hangovers. Answering the phone, he mumbled, "Hunh?" His lips weren't working so well, either.

"Merry Christmas, Joshua!" exclaimed Scott. Joshua had to hold the receiver away from his ear to lessen the pain of the noisy greeting. "Sabrina told me to call you and invite you for breakfast. Bloody Mary's, cheesy eggs, sausage, and gravy and biscuits."

"Hold on." Joshua raced to his kitchen sink in the nick of time, where he disgorged the limited contents of his stomach.

"Dude, are you alright?"

"Uh. Not feeling very well, man. I need to go back to bed."

"OK, OK, but you are missing a great Christmas morning breakfast!"

"See ya'," Joshua mumbled and, as he tried to hang up the phone, missed the phone's cradle. The loud clatter as it hit the floor added more excruciating pain to his head. He slowly trudged up the stairs to the bathroom, where he ran a sink of cold water. Taking a deep breath, he plunged his face into the water and held it there as long as possible. Taking another deep breath, he again baptized his aching head.

He thought about taking some aspirin, but he knew he would not be able to hold it down. His head was killing him, his mouth tasted like death, and he desperately needed some water. Easing himself into his bed, he thought that maybe he should have gone to church with Miss Flo and Mr. Frankie instead of going to the church of Jim Beam. Eventually, he fell asleep.

Later, he slowly woke up and became conscious of three things. The first was that his head still hurt badly, but it was better. Second, he heard the drip, drip of rain in the gutters, but he also heard tick ticking against the window. The third thing was more alarming. He heard something whining and snuffling against the back door. The sound was pitiful.

Slowly and carefully, holding his head stiffly to prevent further pain, he descended the stairs. He opened the door and was surprised to see a puppy. The little coal black dog was shivering and whining against the cold wind, rain, and sleet. It was way too thin, its belly protruding like a starving refugee. He beckoned to the dog to come in; it needed no further encouragement to waddle inside. Shutting the door quickly against the cold, Joshua took a kitchen hand towel and began to rub the puppy dry. Then, he wrapped him in a blanket from the couch and laid him on the rug in front of the gas space heater, which he turned on high.

Joshua went into the kitchen to scrounge up something for it to eat. Looking in the refrigerator, he saw that he had eggs and butter, so he set about to scramble some eggs on his gas stove. He put some of the eggs on a saucer and took it to the dog. The puppy roused and began to devour the eggs. Unfortunately, they did not stay down. It had been too long since he had eaten.

"Let's try some water then," Joshua said. He filled a bowl with water, which the puppy eagerly lapped up. Again, it would not stay down. He cleaned up both messes and realized he would need to take it very slowly. So, he placed just a spoon of eggs on a plate, and this time, it stayed down. Then, he gave the dog a few teaspoons of water in the bowl, and it too stayed down.

A rumble of hunger moved through Joshua's stomach, and he took that as a good sign. Having learned from his experience with the pup, he ate only a few bites and took only a couple of sips of water. He settled on the couch to watch his visitor, hoping that his sustenance would stay down long enough to take some aspirin. When his stomach settled, he drank some of his leftover Coke, took two aspirin, and ate the remainder of the eggs.

With his head finally beginning to feel better, Joshua mused that he was glad the bar was closed for Christmas Day. He decided to turn on his portable radio to check the weather. When it was tuned to the local country station, the first thing he heard was Dolly Parton singing "Hard Candy Christmas." She sang, "Lord it's like a hard candy Christmas / I'm barely getting through tomorrow...."

"Well, that fits, doesn't it?" he said to the orphaned puppy. He picked up the empty whiskey bottle, strode to the kitchen, and dumped it in the trashcan with a crash.

As Dolly's song concluded on the radio, the DJ chimed in, "Well, hope you are ready for a 'Hard Candy Christmas' cause it looks like we have an ice storm headed our way! Might lose power. Better get down to Jitney Jungle tomorrow to get that milk and bread while you can, cause the freeze should start in the afternoon. And tell those good folks down at Jitney Jungle that Steve Malone sent you! And while you're at it, tell 'em Merry Christmas!"

CHAPTER NINETEEN
"Winter Wonderland"

Joshua was glad he listened to Steve Malone on the radio. When stores opened after noon on Sunday, he went out for supplies, but not to Jitney Jungle. He knew it would be a madhouse. Instead, he puttered down to the Gibson Discount Center for supplies. Fortunately, his apartment had gas space heaters, a gas stove, and a gas hot water heater, so he could stay warm, cook, and bathe. He would just need light and a place to keep water, in case the pressure went down with a prolonged power outage.

He brought home a Coleman lantern with extra mantles and fuel, a couple of flashlights with batteries, and batteries for his portable radio. "Let there be light!" he said grinning. He also purchased a five gallon water container with a built-in faucet like campers and fishermen use. He would fill that up and put it next to the kitchen sink for washing up in case he lost water. He would also fill up the bathtub with water for the toilet, just like they used to do with snowstorms back in North Carolina.

For food, he kept it simple, realizing that without power and his refrigerator, he didn't need to buy anything fresh. So, cans of Dinty Moore beef stew, Hormel chili, various soups, Vienna sausages, and Spam went into his shopping cart. He also bought crackers, bread, and a six pack of Bud. Thinking he would need some fruit and vegetables, he threw in some canned green beans and English peas, along with canned peaches, pears, and fruit cocktail. He couldn't resist a box of Little Debbie oatmeal cakes for comfort food. He didn't forget the puppy, either. He grabbed a bag of Puppy Chow, a chew toy, a collar, and a leash. On the way out he bought the Sunday paper for house training. With these items in his VW, he headed home, but not before he stopped to fill up with gas. You never know.

And now, as he looked out his sub-basement windows at the "Winter Wonderland," he was glad he went out. The limbs on nearby trees were covered in a thin layer of ice, and they bent down under the weight. Walking up to the front porch of the house, he could see that the street was icing over, as were the power lines and phone lines. And still, the freezing rain came. It was beautiful and peaceful in one sense, but terrible in another. The only sound one could hear was the tinkling of the rain and the sighing of the wind. Suddenly, there was a loud crack, like a shot, followed by a loud crash. A large branch across the street took down a power line, and that was when the lights went out.

Joshua used the light from the sub-basement windows to prep and fire up the Coleman lantern. And the puppy? Well, he seemed content to lie in front of the heater. Joshua fed him, but he was careful to give him only a little at a time, so he would not gorge himself. When the weather cleared, Joshua planned to check with his neighbors to see who was missing a puppy. In the meantime, he had to admit that he was a sweet little fella'. And who knew when the weather would clear?

As if the announcer on the radio heard Joshua's thoughts, he said, "Well, folks, looks like the ice storm will end tonight - but hold on! The US Weather Service has informed us that another front is on the way, and it will likely bring snow! After that, the temps will plunge for a few days. This is unprecedented in this part of Mississippi, so I hope everyone is prepared."

As if on cue, the phone rang. It was Sabrina with news that the owner had decided to shut down the Boiler Room until further notice. "Do you have everything you need?"

"I'm set," Joshua replied. "How about ya'll?"

"We fought the mobs at the store this afternoon, so we should be OK." Sabrina paused. "How are you?" Their last conversation had been a deep, emotional, and revealing one.

"Actually, I'm OK," he replied, "but thanks for asking."

"I'll let you know when we can reopen," Sabrina said. "This is certainly hurting our business, especially since New Year's Eve falls on a Friday. Hopefully, we can reopen that night and have bowl game specials on New Year's Day to make up for our losses."

No sooner had he hung up the phone than it rang again. The gravelly voice on the other end told him exactly who it was. "Joshua? This is Flo. You doing OK? You got everything you need?"

"Yes, ma'am, but thanks for thinking of me. And I'm sorry if I was rude when you stopped by Christmas Eve. I just wasn't feeling well, but I am better now. How 'bout ya'll?"

"We're good, but the other reason I called is let you know that we cleaned out the fridge down at the restaurant and brought it here. Figured the power would go out. So, tonight, it's all you can eat, burgers and beer! Don't want to let anything go to waste! Darnell has snow chains on his squad car, so he will try to make it up the hill to join us. Why don't you come over around six? We are going to feed the other renters, too."

"That sounds great! Thanks so much! I'll see ya'll then."

***

He did not have to look at the clock to know when it was almost six. Permeating the entire house was the tantalizing aroma of high-quality ground beef sizzling in a cast iron skillet. He took the dog outside for a potty break, being very careful on the slippery ice. Next, he spread fresh newspaper on the floor, put a little chow in a bowl, and tucked the puppy in his blanket in front of the heater. But as he was about to leave, the puppy gave him the most soulful and pitiful look. So, Joshua gave him some gentle ear scratches; the puppy sighed with rapture.

Then, he followed his nose up from his living room to the first-floor hallway. The smell was more intense there. Crossing the hall, he knocked on the door where Miss Flo and Mr. Frankie lived. The door was opened by Darnell, and the smell of burgers from inside had Joshua's stomach rumbling.

"Glad to see you made it up the hill, Triple-D!"

"It was touch and go for sure. I had to take it real slow. If the snow comes like they say it will, I might not make it home, cause going downhill is a different matter. Fortunately, Auntie

Flo and Uncle Frankie have a second bedroom. Can't think of anyone better to hang out with in a storm like this."

"For sure!"

"Anyway," Darnell began, "welcome to the first annual 'Power's Out Party.'" With a sweep of his hand, he ushered Joshua inside, where the living area was lit by two Coleman lanterns and several candles. The furnishings were old but comfortable, with two couches and several lounge chairs. Miss Flo had a portable radio playing old, old country gospel music from a station in Jackson.

There were happy greetings with Miss Flo and Mr. Frankie, and as usual, the burgers were mouth-watering. He declined a beer, however, in favor of Miss Flo's sweet tea. They ate with plates on their laps in the living area. Because he worked at night, Joshua had not met any of his neighbors, who all worked in the daytime. Introductions were exchanged. He met a recent college grad from upstairs who was a rookie reporter at the local paper. She came from Jackson, as did the other upstairs neighbor. He worked as a disc jockey at the local FM station. The other apartment on the first floor, the one between his and the front porch, was shared by two women. They both were in ad sales, one at the paper and the other at the AM station. As Joshua met each of the other housemates, he remembered to ask if anyone had lost a puppy. No one had.

As time went on and more beers were consumed, he noticed that one of the women who shared the first-floor apartment kept looking over at him. She seemed nice and was attractive, but Joshua's heart still belonged to his missing bride. He made a point of holding his tea high with his left hand, so she could see his ring.

Suddenly, someone shouted, "Look out the window!" Everyone jumped up and crowded around the window. Even in the darkness outside, one could see big fat snowflakes swirling down. As they watched, the snow grew thicker, and the wind began to drive the flakes against the windowpanes. It was not the kind of thing that Delta folks got to see often, if at all.

"Well, Triple-D, looks like you will be crashing here tonight," Joshua said.

"No problem. I've got something to show you anyway."

As the party began to break up, Joshua said his farewells. Darnell followed him out the door. Once in Joshua's apartment, Darnell noticed the puppy first thing. "Where did you get this little guy?" he said, crouching to pet the coal black dog.

"He wandered up yesterday. He was freezing in that brutal weather."

"Someone sent you a Christmas present! On the other hand, maybe you are the dog's present!"

"Well, I wouldn't mind keeping him, but I'm going to check around the neighborhood to see if anyone is missing him. And, I need to check with Miss Flo and Mr. Frankie."

"They won't mind."

They settled on the couch, and Joshua said, "So, what is it you want to show me?"

"Thought you might like to see these." From his jacket pocket, Darnell pulled out a packet of pictures.

"My pictures!"

"Yes, and as it turns out, they are very good. The MBI may come knocking on your door with an offer to work undercover. Good job! And yes, I took the liberty of sending them copies."

"Ha! I manage to get into enough trouble as a bartender," Joshua chuckled, "much less working for them. I'm glad you went ahead and sent them in." They spread the pictures out on the coffee table, and they were just as the detective described. It was very easy to identify the two men involved, and it was easy to see exactly what they were doing. "So, what's next?" Joshua asked.

"Well, they need to catch Bubba and his henchman with the goods in their possession. They would like to do a stakeout, but they don't have enough manpower to just wait around. Too easy to be spotted on a long stakeout, anyway. They need a tip as to Bubba's next trip to the Keys."

"I'll try to find out, if I can."

***

Indian Springs wound up with eight inches of snow, and it did not get above freezing for two days. There was no traffic on the road because no one was going anywhere. At first, Darnell and Joshua enjoyed hanging out and swapping stories, but it was not long before they ran out of them. It also didn't take long for Joshua to get sick of the canned food he bought. The confinement grew tiresome after a couple of days, but his boredom was alleviated somewhat by the puppy. Slowly but surely, Joshua paper-trained the dog and worked on teaching it to eat and drink without gorging. It was a work in progress.

Fortunately, the temperature began to rise on Wednesday. The sun was out, and the DOT began to salt and sand the roads. Why so long to do it? Joshua later learned that since the area saw so little snow and ice, they weren't equipped to do much. They had to start with the main roads. He was happy to see they had gotten to the steep street in front. The weatherman said that the sun would be out the rest of the week, and the temperature would rise each day. Thus, the snow began to melt in the streets.

The power came back on in the middle of Thursday night, and Sabrina called him first thing the next morning to see if he could make it to work Friday night. The street in front of the Boiler Room had been cleared, she said, so customers could make it in. For his part, Joshua was happy to have something to do. Sabrina figured the rest of their snowbound regulars would feel the same way. So, she said she would spread the word through the grapevine that there would be a New Year's Eve bash that night with drink specials.

Not long after they opened, the jukebox was thumping, and the Boiler Room was jumping. The regulars weren't used to being cooped up by snow. Business was brisk at the bar, and Joshua and Sabrina stayed "in the weeds," as they say in the trade. Still, Joshua was able to ask most patrons if anyone had lost a dog.

Reuben and Jeff crashed through the door with a bang, ordering beers with a bellow. Not long afterwards, Greg and

Shelley ambled in, looking for a couple of Chardonnays. Next up was Carly Jane Lacy and a couple of the Mindbenders. Joshua had her Jack and Coke ready by the time she made it to the bar. He was in the process of opening some Bud Lights for the boys in the band when she greeted him.

"Hey, Joshua! What's up? Did you like the snow and ice?"

"What do you think? What about you?"

"I hate it! Don't like to be cooped up! Besides, I would rather be in Key West!"

Joshua's ears perked up with the words "Key West." He said, "I bet Key West would be nice about now. It's warming up here, but it's still cold, and there is still snow on the ground."

"Yeah, I wish I could go there with Bubba!"

"Is he there now?"

"Yeah, when he heard that the ice was coming, he packed up and left!"

"Must be nice."

"Yeah," she agreed, sipping her drink, "but I heard he's coming back next Tuesday after New Year's Day."

"How do you know so much about Bubba's calendar, anyway?"

"I have little birdies everywhere," she said and grinned before sauntering off to join her buddies.

He was thinking that being a bartender had it perks when it came to hearing gossip, and the crazy thing about gossip in Indian Springs was that it was usually true. Now he had some information to pass along to Darnell, who could pass it on to the MBI. He called him first thing Saturday morning to share what he learned about Bubba. Darnell said that he would pass the intel along.

Hanging up the phone and looking out the window, Joshua could tell that enough snow had melted so that he would be able to take the dog for a walk. He would have liked to check around the neighborhood to see if the puppy belonged to anyone, but he didn't have time. He needed to hustle to the bar for New Year's Game Day.

CHAPTER TWENTY
A Break in the Case?

They opened early on New Year's Day. Sabrina bustled around the bar, worrying about their dwindling supply of alcohol. They wouldn't be able to get a delivery until Tuesday. Meanwhile, Joshua and Scott wrestled a couple of televisions into the bar and set them up in the area near the pool tables and video games. With rabbit ears, the tv's could pick up the three networks from Jackson. Soon, there were patrons seated in front of them, sipping their beers and watching the Rose Bowl parade. The bowl games would come later.

Sabrina knew that they had to have some kind of snacks, since Le Monde wasn't open this day. So, she directed Scott and Joshua to bring in the theater's popcorn machine. The smell of fresh popping corn soon filled the bar. Sabrina also got permission to use the Le Monde kitchen, and she used it to slow-cook huge pots of black-eyed peas and collard greens, the traditional New Year's meal down South. There were also trays of cornbread. Available for a price, of course, until they ran out.

Once again, the regulars all showed up, and some showed out. Sabrina told Joshua that between last night and today, they just might make up what they lost while closed. The bowl games were a big draw, as were the discounted beer prices. In the "Granddaddy of Them All," the Rose Bowl, UCLA beat Michigan, and then Nebraska edged LSU in the Orange Bowl. At four o'clock, Sabrina and Scott covered one of the pool tables with a tarp and a couple of tablecloths. They used that to set up a buffet, and the hungry men dug in, not taking their eyes off the game. The nightcap was the Sugar Bowl, where legendary coaches Joe Paterno and Penn State faced Vince Dooley and Georgia. The Nittany Lions defeated the Bulldogs in a close one, 27-23. And yes, most of the patrons stayed to the very end, whooping and hollering over good plays and throwing up their hands for bad ones.

The Boiler Room sold a lot of draft beer that day, and the crew went home worn slap out! They cleaned up after the food, but they decided to wait until Tuesday to get the place in order. If they came in early, they could do so and store the alcohol order.

Joshua didn't sleep well that night. He knew that it wouldn't be long before Bubba was due to fly back from Key West. He couldn't help but wonder – and worry – about what would happen. The next morning was a slow one. He didn't realize how tired he was, but he was glad to have two days off in a row. He made breakfast, and afterwards, decided to take the dog for a walk. He knocked on a lot of doors, but a lot of folks were at church. The people he was able to talk to - no one was missing a puppy.

Returning to their warm apartment, Joshua petted the puppy and gave him some food and water. He was still learning to eat and drink appropriately. Joshua slept better that night.

He spent a leisurely Monday stocking up on fresh food and supplies and catching up on cleaning and laundry. Later, he again walked the dog. He knocked on the doors he missed the day before, but again, no one was missing a dog.

"Looks like no one is claiming you, young man," he said to the dog. "I guess you get to be my Christmas present, after all." The puppy wagged its tail happily, and there seemed to be a smile on his face. "What shall I name you? Hmmm."

Tuesday was a busy morning at the bar getting things cleaned up, set up, and put up. Joshua didn't have time to think about what might happen that night with Bubba and the MBI. The evening was slow, however, very slow. Sabrina suggested that the big bashes Friday and Saturday sapped everyone's energy, if not their pocketbooks. Joshua told Sabrina and Scott to go home. Later, as he closed up and drove home, he decided against trying to contact Darnell. He had promised Joshua that he would let him know as soon as he knew. Despite his concerns, Joshua slept deeply and well that evening. He was still recovering from the long days and lack of sleep.

The next night was more of the same, and he still hadn't heard from the detective. He was a little puzzled by that, but he told himself to be patient. However, the phone was ringing when he entered his apartment after closing. It was Darnell, and he asked if he could stop by in a few minutes. "Of course!" Joshua said eagerly. He had a beer ready for him when he walked in. Darnell looked askance at Joshua's glass of ice water. They sat down on the couch, and Joshua said, "Well, what happened?"

Before he could reply, the puppy came bounding up to Darnell, tail wagging. He gave the dog a good rub. "What you gonna' name this dog?" he said with a grin. Joshua shrugged. Then, when the puppy wandered off, he asked again what had happened. Darnell said, "Long story short, something but nothing."

"What?! You're talking in riddles!" Joshua exclaimed impatiently.

"The 'something' is that the MBI was all set to make a bust. They had a scout in a Ghillie suit with night vision binoculars. The rest of the team was staged nearby, waiting, locked and loaded. They even had a helicopter ready to swoop in."

"And?"

"And, that gets us to the 'nothing.' The plane landed, Bubba and his girlfriend got out, but there was no merchandise. Bubba's guard picked them up in the truck, and they drove to the house."

Joshua's stomach fell and he groaned. "The MBI must think I'm an idiot! I should have known it was too good to be true that things could move this swiftly."

"I know you are disappointed but be patient. My contact with the MBI said that they weren't upset. First, I had told them that you were almost caught when you took your pictures. They figured, because of that, Bubba was paranoid. He decided to check things out. A test run, if you will. Since no bust came, he will be overconfident when he makes his next run."

"What's the other thing, the second thing?" Joshua asked.

"The MBI team saw this as a good dry run. They made some mistakes that could have blown the operation. Now, they have a much better idea of how to proceed. They just need a tip about when he's going back to Florida."

"I'll see what I can do. Thanks."

Getting up from the sofa, Darnell said, "Thanks for the beer!" With a wave of his hand, he was out the back door.

***

It was two weeks later before Joshua found out about Bubba's next trip. He didn't even have to ask. Carly Jane came in complaining that Bubba had canceled a party, and the Mindbenders had lost a gig. Bubba had to go out of town "on business." Joshua eagerly passed this information on to Darnell, who in turn passed it on to his contact in the MBI. Once again, it was a waiting game.

In the meantime, the puppy was starting to look more normal – better fed, in other words. The paper training was going so well that there were no longer any accidents on the floor. Joshua was able to take the puppy for a daily walk, where it got in the habit of taking care of business. After throwing away the last of the newspaper, Joshua sat down on the floor with the puppy. When he scratched its ears, the puppy gave him his belly in trust.

"You are turning into a fine dog," he said. "Why would someone turn you out? Or did you just get lost? You look a little like a black lab, but there's something else mixed in there, too." The puppy wagged his tail and grinned. Then, as if in reply, he chuffed three times.

"When I was a kid up in the mountains, I had a dog. I named him 'Puppy.' Not very original, I know, but I loved that dog. All we had to feed him was table scraps. He followed me everywhere. I used to go off into the woods to play frontiersman. I would get a stick and use that as my long gun. I pretended that I was Davy Crockett."

Again, the puppy chuffed three times.

"That dog stayed with me all the time I was playing. Once, he scared off a bobcat that we ran across. I think he was protecting me. He was a good dog. Are you going to be a good dog? Hunh? Are you a good dog?" Joshua playfully wrestled with the puppy, who growled and wriggled and wrestled, as well. "What should I name you, boy? What do you think?"

"Ruff, ruff, ruff!" was the puppy's reply.

"You know, I always liked Davy Crockett. I learned in college that he opposed President Andrew Jackson's 1830 order to remove the Native Americans from the South. That was a brave thing to do, and it cost him politically. That's why he went to Texas, where he died at the Alamo. I guess you could say Davy was a friend to the Cherokee. That was a good thing. Will you take a brave stand someday? Will you be a friend to the Cherokee?"

Three more chuffs followed.

"I think I'll name you Davy Crockett, then. Yeah! How do you like that, hunh? Do you like that? Hmmm?" The puppy said yes in his own puppy way. Three times, in fact.

***

The time passed slowly, and Joshua fretted about the lack of news. Finally, on Friday night, Darnell dropped by the Boiler Room and invited Joshua for a burger at Miss Flo and Mr. Frankie's. Entering the little café, he found the trio sitting around the dilapidated table. The usual greetings were exchanged, along with the food order, and the two owners went to the kitchen to prep the food.

Darnell grabbed two beers from the cooler and plopped them on the table. Pulling the tab on his, he said, "Well?" and nodded at the second beer.

"No thanks," Joshua said.

"Now that's a first, seeing you turn down a beer. Are you counting calories or something?"

"Nah, just slowing down on the intake."

Wondering what that was all about, Darnell grunted.

"Well, anyway, I have some news."

"Good! I was hoping you would. So, what happened?"

"Bubba flew in. He and his helper began to unload their haul, and the MBI swooped in. The operation went like clockwork; not a shot was fired."

"Great! But wait, nobody has said a word about this at the bar, and there has been nothing on the news," Joshua observed.

"And there won't be," Darnell said. "The MBI wants to keep this quiet for now. That means what I'm telling you is privileged. They don't want the FBI involved. They could take over the case since the cocaine crossed state lines. The MBI wants to be able to do things their way."

"Why?"

"This is the part you might not like. They want to offer Bubba a deal."

"Oh, Lord, here we go," Joshua said and huffed.

"I know, I know, but hear me out. There are two reasons for a deal. The biggest reason is that they want to take down the whole operation. They are hoping that Bubba will give up his supplier, as well as the folks he sells to."

"You really think he would give up his supplier? Wouldn't they be some pretty nasty boys from South America?"

"Yeah, you are probably right, but if they get Bubba and his buddy to sell the coke to his dealers, they can at least take all of them down in drug raids."

"You said there was a second reason to keep it quiet?"

"Wel-l-l-l-l, Bubba is pretty well connected down in Jackson. He has 'friends' that don't want this to come to light. It could embarrass a lot of important people. They think some of Bubba's connections might be using themselves."

"So, he would just get off Scott-free?"

"No, no, no, no! They have already confiscated the coke, his plane, his big truck, and his farm. They have seized his bank accounts, and he will lose his licenses to practice law and fly a plane. He will serve five to seven years in prison, probably in a minimum-security facility."

"And the rest of the men will wind up in Parchman Farm, while the rich man gets to cool out in a country club prison."

"That's one way to look at it," the detective agreed. "But the other way is to take the win. A big cocaine operation in the Delta would be put out of business. Probably for good."

Joshua huffed.

"There's one other thing the MBI is asking in exchange for the deal. They want Bubba to agree to being questioned by me about Dee Dee's murder."

Joshua brightened. "Now, we're talking! When will that happen?"

"First, he has to take the deal."

"Oh. And where is he now?"

"That I don't know. All I know is that he is being held without bail – for now."

CHAPTER TWENTY-ONE
Movement

Late January in the Delta can be depressing. Cloudy, foggy, rainy, and cold – just miserable. Most folks avoided being out in the weather whenever they could: they hustled to work and then hustled home at the end of the day, where they stayed in their warm, dry living rooms. Naturally, business at the Boiler Room was slow, so Joshua and Sabrina were taking more time off. For Joshua, who was waiting to find out what happened with Bubba Bryce, the hours seemed to drag by. He could only read so much. On the other hand, it was a good time to train Davy Crockett. Before long, he had learned to "sit" and to "stay." It didn't take long for the pup's name to become, simply, Davy.

There was a little more action on one "Thirsty Thursday," so both Sabrina and Joshua were working. During one lull in the action, Scott burst through the theater's dressing room door. Taking a seat at the bar, he ordered a beer and asked Joshua how it was going.

The bartender cracked open the canned beer and placed it on a paper coaster on the bar. "Not much happening here," Joshua replied as he wiped down the bar. "Say, I was wondering what show you are going to do next."

Scott looked at him dolefully. "I don't really know. To be honest, I don't have a lot of good ideas right now."

"Don't ya'll normally do a spring show?"

"Yes, but…." Scott acted like he wanted to continue, but he was watching Sabrina, who was taking out a tray of mugs to wash. When she was gone, he said, "Don't say anything about what I'm about to tell you, okay?"

"Sure."

"I don't know if we are going to be able to stay in Indian

Springs much longer."

"Why?"

"It's the whole Dee Dee thing," Scott said and sighed. "It has been really weighing on Sabrina. The gossip, the stares. I don't know if she can take it much longer. She wants me to start looking for a job somewhere else."

"Oh man, I'm sorry to hear that! What would the theater, and for that matter the bar, do without you two?"

"I don't know. I don't really want to go, but I don't want Sabrina to have to deal with this much longer. It's like we're living under a cloud, waiting for the ax to fall."

Joshua would have chuckled at the mixed metaphor, but considering the gravity of the situation, he remained sober faced. He knew what Scott meant, and he knew how serious things were.

"They need to find out who did it, so she can get her life back."

Isn't that the truth, Joshua thought. I would like that, too.

***

At last, the wait was over for intel. Darnell showed up at Joshua's apartment the next Sunday afternoon. Skipping the formalities, he got straight to the point. "Well, Bubba rejected the plea deal."

Joshua threw up his hands in frustration.

"The case is moving forward, nonetheless."

"In what way?"

"Seems like our friend Mr. Bryce figured something was up if they were offering him a deal. He probably realized that his friends in high places were a plus, so he negotiated. The State DA balked at first, but he eventually accepted Bubba's proposal."

"And what would that be?"

"He will not be required to give up the name of his South American supplier, but he will give up the names of the dealers he had been selling the coke to. However, he won't have to be a part of any MBI's sting on them."

"So far, I'm with you. What else?"

"He gets to keep his farm, and he will serve three to five years in a country club prison."

"Good grief!"

"I know you think he's getting off light but think about it. He will not be able to practice law again, and he may never get back his pilot's license. They took his truck and his coke. They also took his money, so unless he has money stashed in some place like the Bahamas, he's broke. If he can't pay his property taxes, he could lose the farm eventually, anyway. That's a big deal: that farm has been in his family for generations. To me, the best part is that the MBI will be able to shut down coke sales in the Delta."

"But he could be back in business in as little as three years."

"I don't think he's that big of a fool. All eyes will be on him. Even his friends at the state level don't want to see that happening. He's going to have to be a farmer like his daddy and granddaddy, IF he can somehow save the farm."

"What about the part where you get to interview him? Is that off the table, also?"

"No, that's a go."

"OK, I'm starting to feel a little better about things. When can you interview him?"

"Going to Jackson tomorrow."

"Good luck! There are a lot of people dealing with this. Hope you get something concrete!"

***

Unfortunately, he did not. Or so it seemed at first. Darnell gave Joshua the scoop over a cheeseburger Wednesday night at Miss Flo and Mr. Frankie's place.

"I can't tell you how long I've been waiting to hear this," Joshua said, ignoring his burger. Darnell did not ignore his. Between bites, he revealed what he had learned.

"Best if I give you the long version, what I learned from the MBI, so you can get the context of all this."

"OK."

"Bubba had been a very successful lawyer in Jackson. When his father died, he went back to the farm to take care of things. It didn't take him long to realize that his dad was in massive debt trying to grow cotton. So, he switched to soybeans - cheaper and more stable - but not a way to get out of debt. To put his problems on the back burner, he started to party a lot. He wound up growing his own grass to party with his friends. Eventually, he began to deal."

"How did he get away with that? Doesn't the state have helicopters and stuff to look for the plants?"

"Well, he converted some shotgun shacks on his property to greenhouses to hide it. Simply replaced the roofs with those clear, fiberglass panels. The light could get to the plants, but the plants couldn't be seen from the air because of the sun's glare on the roofs. Furthermore, he wasn't using grow lamps, so the choppers couldn't pick up the heat signal via infrared sensors."

"Pretty smart."

"With his ability to grow more grass, he became a big distributor. It helped him pay some of his daddy's bills. Then, through drug dealers he had defended, he got connected to some Louisiana boys and coke. So, on a trip with his girl to the Florida Keys, he would land on a grass strip near Everglade City and meet the bullet boats at night. He flew some to a private strip outside of Shreveport and some to Memphis via a private landing strip outside of Oxford. The rest he brought here. As coke became more lucrative, he backed off selling grass. And by selling coke, he paid off his dad's bills."

"Interesting stuff, but how about Dee Dee's murder?"

"We're getting there. Here's what I learned from him. Turns out, his business was so profitable, he could afford to loan money. Here's where it gets interesting. He loaned money to Paul Scarborough. Turns out Paul was deep in debt from gambling and he and Bubba's uncle were Ole Miss frat boys together."

"So, that's how he remained in good standing with the casino and his bank. Bubba fronted him the money to pay up." Darnell nodded yes. "But how is this connected to Dee Dee? Wait!

If Paul couldn't pay up, Bubba could have sent his bodyguard to threaten him, and his family! Or, to kill Dee Dee. That's why he and Paul were arguing at the Deer Party!"

"Exactly. So I asked him. He said that he did send his bodyguard to 'shake Paul up,' but he never threatened Dee Dee or Haley. He said he had nothing to do with Dee Dee's murder."

"Do you believe him?"

"Actually, I do. I don't see him needing the money back that badly. And, he has a solid alibi to boot, as does his bodyguard."

"Fair enough, but what if he did send that guy to threaten Dee Dee, and something went wrong?"

"I asked him about that as well."

"What did he say?"

"Never happened. And before you ask, I believe him."

"So, for all this work and effort, we got nothing! I feel like an idiot sneaking onto his farm to take pictures and stuff. That was stupid."

"Not exactly. He did give me one important piece of info."

"Yeah, what's that?"

"He told me that Paul did repay him."

"How was he able to do that?"

"That's a good question. My first thought was Dee Dee's insurance policy."

"I don't know, man. I don't see Paul killing Dee Dee. He seemed to have really loved her."

"Yeah, but desperate men do desperate things."

"I guess. So, you have a bullseye on Paul now?"

"I will interview him again. I think that, with this intel, the chief will let me press him a little more. Check on the beneficiary of Dee Dee's life insurance policy, for example. Double check his alibi. But, I'm not giving up on other possibilities."

So, Sabrina is still under the gun, Joshua thought. Dang!

"He did tell me one other interesting thing. He said that if we didn't think Paul murdered Dee Dee for the money, there was one other way he could have gotten the money to pay Bubba back."

"What was that?"

"He said maybe we should check the books at the refinery that Paul runs."

Joshua huffed. "I'm surprised he would give Paul up like that."

"Remember you told me how Paul was arguing and poking him in the chest at the Deer Party? There's no love lost there. I also got the impression that Bubba thinks Paul 'narked' on him to the MBI."

"Doesn't it get exhausting chasing down all these leads?" Joshua asked. "I'm worn out just thinking about it!"

"So much for you being a detective, bud," Darnell said and laughed. "But yes, it does. However, that's the only way to solve a case. Now, finish your burger!"

"Thanks for keeping me in the loop."

"You bet but remember to keep your mouth shut!"

"Copy. Remember, bartenders are good at listening, not talking."

***

Jan-u-ugly turned to Feb-u-weary. No relief in sight from the dismal weather. And it seemed to affect everyone, but especially Sabrina. Not even the music at the bar could cheer her up. Joshua had insisted on putting some new music on the jukebox. "You Were Always on My Mind" by Willie Nelson was playing as she walked in.

"Sabrina! How's it going?"

She flipped open the countertop wearily, gave him a "leave-me-alone" look, and ambled behind the bar. Her face looked as dreary as the weather. Joshua was thinking he needed to do something to cheer her up.

"Ok, lady," he began, "you wouldn't leave me alone at Christmas until I spilled the beans, so out with it. What's wrong."

Sabrina sullenly looked at him a beat and then said,

"Fair enough. It's just this Dee Dee Scarborough thing. She overshadows everything, even now in her death."

"What do you mean?'

"I'm still a suspect, stupid!" she blurted. Realizing her temper had flared, she took a deep breath and then said, "Wait. Wait. Sorry about the 'stupid.' I'm just so frustrated. It's like I told you before, every time I turn around that detective seems to pop up."

"No worries. I can't imagine what that must be like."

"I need a vacation or something. Maybe it's time for us to move on. It's like my reputation here is shot to hell."

Joshua desperately wished he could share what he knew with her, but he had given his word. Even so, he didn't have any real news.

Trying to cheer her up, Joshua said, "You just need to take a break. Do something fun. I heard on the radio that REO Speedwagon is gonna' be in Jackson March 16th. Maybe we should get a crew together and go."

"I do like a couple of their songs."

"Yeah. Good stuff. Let's plan on it."

"Maybe," she said and then walked away towards the dressing room door in the back. As she went looking for Scott, a new song blasted from the jukebox. It was an appropriate one, Joshua thought. "Should I Stay or Should I Go" by the Clash, a song that described her feelings perfectly.

Not long after she left, Carly Jane popped in. "Hey, Joshua! What do you think I want?"

Joshua grinned. "Well, since we don't have what you really want, I'll serve you a Jack and Coke, but where are the boys in the band?"

"They're rehearsing in our garage. I can only take so much!'

"What's been going on?" he asked.

"Not much with me, but hey! Have you heard about Bubba Bryce?"

His ears pricked up, and he said, "No, what?"

"He's disappeared, man!"

"What do you mean?"

"I mean, like disappeared. Off the face of the planet!"

"How do you know?"

"Well, none of us have heard from him for a while. One of our mutual friends even drove out to Bubba's place to check on him. He said the place was deserted. His plane and his truck were gone. It was like he had left in the middle of the night."

Truer words have never been spoken, Joshua thought. "What do you think is going on?"

"I don't know, but it's not like Bubba to just leave like this without telling at least someone."

"Well, you know him better than me, but if I had his money and that plane, I wouldn't be hanging out around here in February. Not when the Coast or the Keys are calling."

"Maybe you are right," she agreed, sipping her drink.

***

As February drew to a close, the weather did begin to warm up somewhat. It was certainly more comfortable to take Davy for his walk. One morning as he did so, the sun was actually out. Joshua reveled in the purple crocus and yellow jonquils that were popping up. He was thinking that Spring might come soon. Even Davy had a pep in his step. Time is so funny, Joshua thought. Seemed like only yesterday that the dog showed up in his life, yet the last two months had drug by. Speaking of time, he realized that it was probably time to get the dog's shots. He was able to get in to see the Vet sooner than he thought he would.

Davy was excited as they walked into the Vet's office, his tail wagging and his eyes sparkling, doggie smells overwhelming his senses. He was a good boy in the waiting room, however. A good chance to practice "sit!" When their turn came to see the vet, he was greeted by a smiling young woman. An attractive young woman. He assumed that she was a vet tech.

"Hi! I'm Doctor West!" she announced as she guided them into the examination room. "What a cute doggie!" she grinned, scratching Davy behind the ears. He responded with three very happy chuffs. "What's your name?"

"This is Davy. Davy Crockett," Joshua said. For his part, he was a bit embarrassed to realize he had fallen prey to a stereotype. But there on the wall was her degree from Mississippi State's vet school. Dr. Leah West, it read. Still, not many female vets now-a-days, he reasoned, cutting himself some slack.

"What a cute name! Is he the 'king of the wild frontier?'" she asked.

"He thinks he is."

"And his chart says you are Joshua MacMillan, his owner?" He nodded yes. "Nice to meet you! So, what can I do for ya'll?"

"Just a check-up and his puppy shots, I guess."

"No problem. How did you come to find such a good-looking pup?"

"He found me. It was Christmas morning. He just wandered up. I checked everywhere, but no one was missing him. I guess he was my present from Santa."

"Looks like he knew just where to go," she smiled, a flirtatious twinkle in her eye.

Joshua froze. Yes, she was very attractive, long dark hair and deep dark eyes. Clearly smart with a good sense of humor, but even thinking such things still felt like a betrayal to Addie. She had been gone over two years now, but was she really gone? The notion of asking someone out made him feel even more guilty.

Fiddling with the ring on his hand, he said, "Yes, it was like he was looking just for me."

Doctor West meticulously checked Davy over and then seamlessly gave him his vaccines. He didn't flinch but continued to grin as only dogs can, wagging his tail happily.

"Such a good dog!" the Vet said. Looking to Joshua, she asked, "Any questions?"

"I guess not."

"Might want to think about getting him fixed in a couple

of months. If you need anything, feel free to call." The same twinkle was in her eyes.

"Thanks!"

Fortunately, the visit was over, and Joshua and Davy were able to beat a hasty retreat.

CHAPTER TWENTY-TWO
"Should I Stay, or Should I Go?"

The last Sunday in February, Darnell came knocking on Joshua's door. As he came into the living room, Davy bounded up to him, happily receiving friendly scratches behind his ears. He panted merrily, his tail wagging like a force of nature.

"This dog is growing up fast," Darnell said as he plopped down on the couch.

"Yes, he is. A far cry from when he showed up, that's for sure. Can I get you a beer?"

"Only if you'll have one with me."

"Sure!" he said as he went to the fridge in the kitchen. He returned with two cold bottles, the lids popped off. "So, what brings you here? Wait, do you have news?"

"Yes, I'm fine," Darnell said sarcastically. "Thanks for asking."

"Sorry."

"No worries. I know you're dying to hear."

"So spill it! Did you interview Paul? What's the latest?"

"Yes, I was able to talk to him, without his lawyer, believe it or not. I asked him again about his alibi. If you remember, he said he was watching TV with Haley at the time of the murder."

"Right. Right."

"I asked if he had anyone else who could substantiate that. As it turns out, he could. Seems that a business associate called during that time, and they talked for half an hour. I talked to that guy, and he was able to confirm. He called Paul at his home phone, and Haley even remembered answering."

"So, doesn't sound like he's the guy."

"No. He was even willing to show me Dee Dee's will when I asked. Turns out she left everything to Haley. Airtight. No one can touch it until she is ready for college. At that point, it pays for schooling each year as long as she is on track to graduate." Joshua huffed. "And when she graduates, she gets one-third of what's left. She gets it all at 25. But, she gets nothing until she's 25 if she doesn't go to school."

"Smart of Dee Dee," Joshua began, "but that means Paul had no motive and no opportunity. So, I guess we're back to square one," he said, realizing unhappily that Sabrina was likely back in the spotlight. "Still, I wonder how he got that money to pay back Bubba Bryce."

"Me, too."

"Are you going to sit on Bubba's suggestion to check Paul's books, or are you going with it? Seems a shame since he's already lost his wife. If he's guilty of embezzlement, he would lose his freedom, as well as Haley."

"He should have thought of that. Unfortunately, I have a duty to uphold the law. I have to report the tip to the MBI."

"And what now?"

"I guess it's back to the 'usual suspects.'"

And that means Sabrina, Joshua mused. Man! Darnell can't find the killer, and Sabrina can't catch a break!

***

Joshua's plans to go see REO Speedwagon did not work out quite as he planned. The night of the concert was a Wednesday, a slow night, but still, someone had to work the bar. He decided it should be him. Sabrina debated with him about that, since she was not really in the mood to party. However, Joshua prevailed. He was able to get four tickets, and he gave them to Sabrina, Scott, Greg, and Shelly as a thank you for their friendship.

Sabrina was late coming in on Thursday, understandably, but she was smiling, bubbling even.

"How was it?" Joshua asked.

"It was great! Just the tonic I needed. We ate before at this nice new restaurant – Nick's. Our seats at the concert were great – thanks again for springing for those. The band was really good. We found ourselves dancing a lot. I like their songs from their

"Hi-Infidelity" album, like 'Keep on Loving You' and 'Take It on the Run.'"

"I'm so glad it was fun for you guys! But, are you ready for 'Thirsty Thursday'?"

"Not really, but we slept in after getting home late. A big breakfast, coffee with a couple of aspirin, and a side of water helped!"

As the two got busy with bar prep, their conversation faded. They hardly noticed when the door opened, and Detective Darnell Dupont walked in. Their happy mood quickly changed. The detective nodded at Joshua and then to Sabrina. When he spoke, his words pierced like a sharp thorn.

"Sabrina, I'm gonna' need you to come downtown with me. I've got some questions."

Alarm registered on her face, and in anger, she blurted, "I'm not talking to you again without my husband and a lawyer present. I'm sick and tired of your harassment, your suspicions! You need to find the real killer and leave me alone!"

"We are working on that. Bring Scott and your lawyer down to the station tomorrow morning."

With a nod to them both, he turned and left quietly. Turning to Sabrina, Joshua thought, so much for brightening her outlook with a fun concert. She flopped into a chair, covered her eyes with both hands, and began to cry. Joshua eased over to her, resting a hand on her shoulder.

When she had somewhat regained her composure, he said. "Why don't you go on home. I can cover tonight." Sabrina did not argue. Instead, she stood up slowly and walked stiffly out the door to the parking lot, her mind far, far away.

"Dang it!" Joshua muttered angrily. "Why did it have to be tonight, Darnell!"

Of course, that was when the crowds showed up, and Joshua was "in the weeds" most of the night. It was later when things had slowed a bit that Carly Jane bounced in. He placed her drink on the bar as she pulled up her chair.

"Hey! You by yourself tonight?" she asked. Joshua nodded

yes but made no comment about Sabrina's absence. "Humph! Thursday is usually busy, right?"

Changing the subject, he said, "So what's new with you?"

"Not much. Did you hear about Paul Scarborough, though?"

"No, what?" he replied, pulse quickening.

"Yeah, I heard he got arrested."

"Really!? What for?" he asked cagily, knowing the likely answer.

"I haven't heard what it was for, but man, that's big news! Do you think they got him for Dee Dee's murder?"

"Anh, I don't see it, but you never know," he said, trying to hide what he knew.

"Well, if it is, it's about time. It's been, what? Eight months?"

"Something like that, I guess."

"I guess we'll find out eventually."

"Maybe so," he said, knowing he needed a cheeseburger after work.

***

When Joshua walked into Miss Flo and Mr. Freddie's place later that night, Darnell was sitting alone at the table. "I've been expecting you," he said. "Your burger has already been ordered."

"Thanks, but man, what's going on? You are questioning Sabrina in the morning, and I just heard that Paul Scarborough has been arrested."

"I guess that bartending thing does put you in a position to hear and see a lot."

"Cut the crap, Darnell. What gives?"

Noting Joshua's tone, he said, "Calm down. Let me explain. I know you are close to Sabrina. Maybe too close and too close to this case."

Joshua huffed and relaxed a bit. "You might be right. Let's start with Paul."

"Yes, I turned the tip over to the MBI, and they audited the books at the refinery. They found solid evidence that he had been embezzling money."

"Did you hear how much?"

"Let's just say it was enough to pay a lot of gambling debts."

"So, what happens now?"

"He will get out on bond in a couple of days. He will be able to keep Haley for now, at least until his trial."

"Man, this sucks for Haley."

"Yes, it does, it really does."

"How much time will he have to serve?"

"Hard to say. Five years, ten? Could be up to twenty."

"Ouch! Haley could be grown and gone by the time he gets out."

"It depends on the judge, the jury, and how good his lawyer is. If he pleads guilty to prevent a trial, he might get five to seven. And he might just wind up in a cell next to Bubba Bryce, for all we know. That would be ironic, wouldn't it?"

"Yep. It's crazy how all this has turned out. Trying to catch Dee Dee's murderer has led to a major drug bust, and a prominent citizen is going to prison for embezzlement. Talk about your unintended consequences. I should have never gotten involved in this thing!"

"But you did. And for your help, blundering as it might have been, the citizens of the state of Mississippi thank you, or they would if they knew. I'm thankful."

"Thanks, but I don't think you could include Paul, Bubba, and his bodyguard Dwayne in with the thankful group."

"No, and that's why I would advise you to continue to keep your mouth shut."

"OK, copy that. But what about Sabrina? She has been wrecked by all this."

"I know. And to be honest, just between the two of us, I don't think she did it. No evidence, really."

"Then why are you questioning her in the morning?"

"Due diligence. We are under pressure from the mayor to solve this problem, believe it or not. Now that he knows that he doesn't have to protect Paul anymore, he's all gung-ho to make a splash. And yes, before you ask, he knows about Paul's alibi and so forth."

"I had no idea that police work could be so political."

"Ha! Dude, you don't know the half of it. I would think that after being in 'Nam you would understand that everything involving money and power gets political."

"Well, this has been a wake-up call for sure. Do you, by chance, have any other leads for Dee Dee's murderer?"

"The official answer is yes, but the truth is no."

Joshua sighed, and just then, Miss Flo brought them their food. "Hey, sugar," she said in gravelly voice. "Good to see you! Don't be a stranger!"

"Yes, ma'am," he said, eyeing his plateful of food. He dug in.

***

Sabrina did not come to work the next day, Friday. Instead, Scott came in her place.

"How's Sabrina?" Joshua asked.

"She's torn up. The detective was relentless with his questions. I'm just glad we had a lawyer there. Without him there, she might have confessed to anything to get it over with."

"That bad?"

"Yeah. Our lawyer told us afterwords that the cops are under a lot of pressure to solve this, so they are turning over every rock. You wouldn't believe how personal the questions got. Anyway, he also told us that based on what they were asking, the cops are just fishing. He doesn't think they have anything."

"Well, of course not. They can't, since she didn't do it. So, what happens next?"

"Well, I hate to tell you this right before the Friday night rush, but we're leaving. Sabrina has had enough."

"I really hate to hear that."

"Yeah, like I said, I don't want to leave really, but Sabrina does. She's been after me to apply for other jobs. As it turns out, I've got an interview in Atlanta Monday."

"Really! What for?"

"It's for a job as assistant director slash stage manager at a theater company in the city. Yeah, it could be a good deal. Better pay, a chance to move up, and Atlanta is a really happening city, really growing."

"I would wish you luck, but I don't want to see ya'll go. Would I have heard of this company?"

"Probably not. It's brand new, just opening. It's called the Horizon Theater, and it's located in this hip part of town called Little Five Points."

"Sounds promising."

That was when it hit Joshua that their move, if made, could affect him. Would he still have a job? Would the new manager of the Boiler Room want him to hang around? Like Sabrina and Scott, should he stay, or should he go?

CHAPTER TWENTY-THREE
"Changes in Attitudes, Changes in Latitudes"

Scott got the job in Atlanta, and the couple began making plans to move. Sabrina was very happy. Wondering how Darnell would react to their move, Joshua was surprised that he merely shrugged his shoulders. He explained that since neither Sabrina nor Scott had been arrested, there was nothing he could do to hold them, even if he wanted to, which he didn't. More and more he doubted their guilt.

As for Joshua, Sabrina introduced him to Mr. Joseph Abdallah, the owner of Le Monde and the Boiler Room. He was a friendly, unassuming man with an easy smile, a second-generation immigrant from Lebanon. He insisted that Joshua call him Joseph. The reason for the meeting was simple: he wanted to offer Joshua the job as manager of the bar. Joshua was pleased that Sabrina recommended him. If he took the job, that would mean a pay raise, but it would also mean extra responsibility. Not only would he tend bar, but he would also handle the business side of things. While Joshua ran the bar, Joseph would continue to run Le Monde, his passion.

Joshua accepted with two conditions. First, he wanted Sabrina to train him and help him train new bartenders. That brought him to point number two. He wanted to be able to hire two part-time bartenders, so he would have a little more flexibility with his schedule. Joseph was agreeable as long as the total hours behind the bar for the three workers were no more what Joshua and Sabrina already worked. Joshua agreed. As did Sabrina, even though she was already beginning to pack.

With Scott and Sabrina leaving, there would be a hole in the heart of the theater. The actors were also their friends. The theater company had begun a search for a replacement, but that was going to be a hard pull to find someone as capable as Scott for what they could pay. In fact, they even considered the cost saving measure of using community volunteers to fill the spot. There were some talented folks in Indian Springs, but that was asking a lot. Hopefully, it would be temporary.

For his part, Joshua began to plan a going away party for them. It would probably be held the first Sunday in April, since they were leaving around the middle of the month. That didn't give him much time to plan, but he was confident that everyone would show for the big send-off and that the theater company would spring for the cost. Through Carly Jane, he had already secured the Mindbenders to play. Once those plans were penciled in, he began the task of hiring a couple of employees. Fortunately, that went well. He had no sooner put up a help wanted sign than he had several applicants. Word travels fast in a small town. He hired the two best candidates.

The first of those two was Carly Jane Lacy. He figured she was a natural, born to be a bartender. Quick with a smile, a great laugh, and good with people. She also knew her way around a bar. Maybe too well? As a result, Joshua was quick to tell both hires that there would be absolutely no drinking on the job. Once they closed, they would be entitled to one comp drink, where they could sit for a moment to decompress. But after that, they would have to help clean and restock, which meant they would drive home sober.

The second hire was Jessica Greenhaw, the "Noodle Princess." Joshua was very impressed with her during the interview. She told him that she planned to go to a local junior college in the fall and live at home to save money. She also hoped to save enough to spend her junior and senior years at Mississippi State. She wanted to major in Wildlife Management, which seemed a perfect fit for her. She would need training for mixing drinks, but really, in a bar that sold mostly beer, a touch of wine, and whiskey and coke, that wouldn't be that big of a deal. Sabrina promised to help train both Jessie and Carly Jane with drink orders, food orders, stocking, and cleaning.

As for Joshua, Sabrina began to show him how to order alcohol and which vendors to use. She also gave him a formula she used for knowing how much to order and when. He learned how to tally up each night's take and when and how to take it to the bank. She also showed him which bills to pay and when. Furthermore, she gave him a little advice about supervising employees, which essentially meant that with young employees you could be friendly, but you could not be friends. Be firm but fair. No excuses for mistakes. Only one second chance. Seemed fair to him.

***

A week of training passed, and Joshua began to feel pretty good about his new hires. Sure, there had been a few bumps along the way: mixed up food and drink orders and a few spilled drinks and broken glasses. However, those minor losses were more than made up for with increased business. There seemed to be more young fellows hanging out than before, and Joshua reflected that neither of his two young hires were hard to look at. His instincts about Carly Jane had been correct. She was a natural. As for Jessie, she made up for her learning curve by outworking everyone. It wouldn't be long before Sabrina would no longer be needed for training, so she could concentrate on packing. Scott had already returned to Atlanta and found a place for them to rent.

The next Saturday night rolled around, and Joshua decided it would be good to have all hands on deck, including Sabrina, just in case. As Joshua was refilling the beer cooler, he heard a unique sound. It was the tap-clacking of someone wearing taps on their shoes. Looking towards the sound, he saw the wearer of those shoes. Boots actually. Fake alligator skin, pointy-toed cowboy boots. Faded, skin-tight blue jeans and a fraying western shirt. Big cowboy belt buckle. Long, greasy hair pulled back in a ponytail. Scruffy beard desperately in need of a trim. And yet, one could tell that he was once a nice-looking man, before the party wore him down. He took a seat at the bar.

Joshua pushed behind the bar and asked what he could

get him. The man ordered a shot of tequila with a Lite beer back. That's odd, Joshua thought, just like…. That was when he noticed the strong smell wafting from the customer – nicotine and marijuana. Joshua also noticed that his eyes were red and glassy.

"Well, well, well!" the man blurted loudly. "I always wondered what the inside of this bar looked like. What a dump!"

Joshua ignored the insult and began to wipe down the bar. For his part, the customer slammed the tequila, grabbed the beer, and swaggered like a movie cowboy towards the pool tables in the back, his taps clacking as though they were saying, "Look at me! Look at me!" Sabrina, who was seated at a table with Scott, had taken all this in. The two new bartenders didn't notice, as they were bussing tables. Sabrina gave Joshua a look and walked up to the bar.

"Who is that?" Joshua began.

"That, sir, is the ex-husband of one Dee Dee Scarborough."

"No way!"

"Oh yeah! His name is Johnny Dix."

"Wow. I would have thought that Dee Dee had more class than that."

"There's no accounting for taste. Still, he was probably good looking as a teenager. People change, or things change them."

"That's for sure," Joshua agreed.

Later, Dix sauntered up to the bar for a refill, before returning to the pool tables. It was not long afterwards that everyone in the bar turned their heads towards a disturbance in the back. There was the sound of arguing, which soon escalated to yelling. Joshua saw Johnny Dix, pool cue in hand, in another man's face. The other man was gesturing wildly, and it looked like a fight was coming. Joshua hustled towards the commotion, palms up in a placating gesture. Approaching the two men, he spoke over the volume of their argument.

"Gentlemen! Let's settle down now. We are all here to have a good time!"

Dix snarled. "You need to mind your own business! This ole boy was trying to cheat me!"

"No, I wasn't!" the other man interjected.

"Well, whatever the case may be, let's tone it down, OK?"

"Whatever, I need another drink anyway," he blurted as he turned and cowboy-swaggered to the bar. "Give me a damn tequila and a Lite beer," he yelled at Sabrina.

Joshua could tell Sabrina was sizing up the situation. Should she serve him or show him the door?

"C'mon!" Dix shouted. "I ain't got all night. I'm here to celebrate!"

Stalling for time, Sabrina said, "What are you celebrating?"

"I am about to get custody of my baby girl that no-good Paul Scarborough would never let me see. Now that he's bound for prison, Haley will be mine again!"

For his part, Joshua felt a pang of guilt and remorse for poor Haley. He walked towards the bar to join Sabrina.

"OK, Johnny. I think you've had enough. Maybe it's time for you to head on home," Sabrina said.

"Don't tell me when I've had enough. I am a paying customer, and I have a right to have a drink!"

Joshua eased up to him and said quietly, "Don't make us call the police, Johnny."

"Who are you talking to me like you know me. You better get out of my face!"

"Let's go," Joshua said, taking Dix by the arm and herding him towards the door.

Dix snatched his arm away and slammed open the door. "All right, I'm going!"

To be sure that he was leaving, Joshua followed him outside, but not before telling Sabrina to call Reuben and Jeff. Once outside, Dix cold-cocked him. The blow stunned Joshua, but he recovered quickly with a one-two combination that took the wind out of Dix. Army training had its benefits. Restraining the angry man, he half- carried, half-marched him through the parking lot. Dix struggled to get free and swung again, but Joshua ducked and continued to follow the retreating man to his battered pickup. Dix snatched open the door and jumped inside. That was when Joshua was surprised to see a gun pointing in his face.

"Listen, big man! If you ever mess with me again, it'll be the last time you ever mess with anyone!"

Joshua held up hands again, palms out. For one or two beats, he wasn't sure what Dix would do.

"All right, just go!" he spat out.

It worked. Dix fired up his truck and slammed it into gear. His tires barked and spun, spewing smoke, as he raced out of the parking lot. The sound of a police siren reached Joshua's ears, and looking towards the sound, he saw the flashing lights of a speeding patrol car. In seconds, it sped past the bar in pursuit of the truck.

Joshua turned and walked back into the bar. As he did so, all eyes were on him. Nonetheless, he calmly moved behind the bar to resume his work.

"What happened out there? Looks like you're gonna' have a shiner in the morning," Sabrina said. Joshua filled her in, and her eyes widened when he mentioned the gun. "I have to admit, I'm a little impressed," she said, gazing at his bruised knuckles. You handled that pretty well."

His checks reddening, he said, "Thanks!"

"We don't usually get this type of behavior in here. We're not like that redneck joint on the other side of town. I hope Reuben and Jeff slam his butt in jail," she snapped.

As it turned out, they did more than just that.

***

A couple of nights later, Reuben and Jeff came in.

"Officers! Greetings! What'll you have?"

"The usual."

"Sure!" As Joshua served up the beers, he said, "Thanks again for your quick response when we had a little trouble here."

"No problem."

"Can I ask how it all turned out?"

"Sure," Jeff said. "That dumb redneck is lucky he's alive. He lost control of his truck on a curve on the highway and wound up in a ditch."

"He was lucky he didn't flip over," Reuben added. "And, of course, he was not wearing a seatbelt."

"He got a few bruises bouncing through the ditch, but he'll live," Jeff continued. "We did a field sobriety test, and it was clear he was at least DUI. We charged him, cuffed him, and put him in the backseat."

"Yeah, he stank of marijuana, so we decided to search the truck," said Reuben.

"What did you find?"

"Let's see," Jeff started. "There was a half-empty bottle of tequila for starters. Open container violation. DUI. Then, we found five bags of grass in a toolbox in the back floorboard."

"Uh-oh!" said Joshua.

"Right. That is possession with intent to sell," explained Reuben.

"Yep," continued Jeff. "Then, we also found a loaded pistol under the seat."

"That would be the one he waved in my face while threatening me," said Joshua.

"Ah, another charge. Making threats with a loaded weapon."

"Yep, and he also punched me."

"That would be assault," said Jeff.

"Where is he now?"

"That clown is still in jail. He couldn't make bail," said Reuben.

"What an idiot," chimed in Jeff.

CHAPTER TWENTY-FOUR
Until Next Time

The day of the farewell party for Sabrina and Scott came. Joshua had worked hard to make this day special. Of course, he had help, especially from Carly Jane and Jesse, but also from Greg and Shelley and Reuben and Jeff. The Boiler Room was nicely decorated, and the theater company had provided snacks and beverages. Friends of the theater and the bar were all present and accounted for. The Mindbenders were playing, couples were dancing, and the bartenders stayed "in the weeds." As Joshua hustled behind the bar to fill orders, he reflected that the party was turning out very well. He did not have time for any sad reflections.

About halfway through the appointed time for the Sunday afternoon party, Greg stood up, quieted the band, and called for everyone's attention.

"Even though today is a sad one," he began, "we have chosen to celebrate Sabrina and Scott." Facing them, he continued," We just want to thank you two for all your contributions to this town and to the theater community. It's been great. Lots of fun. We will miss you, but we refuse to say goodbye. Rather, we say, 'until next time.' And we wish you the best as you move onward and upward in your careers." The crowd erupted in cheers. Then, it was Shelley's turn to speak.

"I'm here to present you with two presents from all of us. The first is this engraved crystal vase to help you remember us." Sabrina and Scott stepped forward to shake hands and receive the gift, to the sounds of hoots and applause. "The second gift is something we hope you enjoy. A three day, all-expenses paid trip to Panama City Beach."

"Man, I want that one!" Carly Jane exclaimed to Joshua

over the cheers.

Then, it was time for Scott to speak. "Ya'll don't know how much this means to us. The presents are very nice, and we thank you, but what means the most is your friendship and the memories of the good times we spent together. We will never forget you, and we hope to simply say, 'until next time.'" Scott swept a tear from his cheek and turned away.

And then from the crowd came the cry, "Sabrina! Speech, speech, speech!"

Tears glistened in her eyes as she came forward. "I don't have a speech. Not really. Let me just echo what Scott said. And, we love you all!" More cheers erupted, and then Greg signaled for the band to play. They broke out a very nice rendition of "You Were Always on My Mind," to which Scott and Sabrina led other couples in a slow dance.

Later, as the party began to wind down, Joshua took a moment to sit with the guests of honor while his two new bartenders attended to the dwindling crowd. Sabrina fixed her eye on Joshua and spoke.

"There is a conversation I need to have with you before we go."

"OK," Joshua replied guardedly.

"I want you to promise me that you will work on moving on with your life."

"That is not so easy. Moving to another town, taking another job – that's easy. Losing the love of your life is hard."

"I'm not going to say I know how you feel, because I don't. I can only imagine what it would be like to lose Scott."

"I hope to God that never happens."

"Me, too. But here's the thing. It's time. You deserve to be happy."

"Not when it was my fault."

"It was not your fault. Addie caught you off-guard and you reacted. Things like that have happened to lots of guys. That has nothing to do with what happened to her. Don't be so hard on yourself."

"Maybe you're right, I don't know. But not knowing what happened to her makes it harder. And what if she is still out there somewhere?"

"What if she is? This may not be what you want to hear, so I will say it gently. I doubt she is alive, but even if she is, she's not with you. She could have found you."

Tears sprang to Joshua's eyes, and he looked away.

"You need to move on. You can start by forgiving yourself. Then, you can begin to let go. Taking that ring off your finger would be a good start."

Joshua looked down at the ring and wondered if he could do that. Could he forgive himself? Could he move on? Then, he spoke.

"One of Addie's favorite poets was John Keats. Do you know him?" They both nodded yes. "So you know that he was a brilliant English poet. He had a promising career ahead of him. He could have been the next Shakespeare, but he got sick. He died of tuberculosis at the age of 25. He died in agony, knowing that his great gift to the world would be wasted."

"I didn't know all of that," Scott said.

"I learned that from Addie. Keats died in Rome. He asked his friends to put something on his tombstone, and it's still there today. It says, 'Here lies one whose name was writ in water.' I'll never forget the day Addie told me about this. We were having a picnic by a mountain waterfall. When she told me about it, I asked her what it meant. She told me to reach over and write her name in the water. No sooner did I form the "A," than it disappeared. Then it hit me. What Keats meant. The impermanence of life. Of how our lives go by so quickly. Of how some are gone too soon."

"Man, that is deep," Scott said. Sabrina's voice caught and tears filled her eyes.

"When Addie told me about Keats, I had a strange premonition. Unfortunately, it turned out to be true. She was like a Cherokee Rose in the spring. A beautiful gift after a cold, lonely winter. Then, she was gone."

"Now I understand," Sabrina said. "It will be hard to move on."

"Yes, but you are right. It's time. Addie taught me that we must make the most of life while we can. 'Carpe Diem.'" Slowly, Joshua reached down and took the ring from his finger and said, "I may take it off, but I'm not going to get rid of it. I will keep it always to remind me of her."

"Then I have a present for you," Sabrina said. She gave him a small box, unwrapped.

Opening it, Joshua was surprised to see a thin, gold necklace. His face lit up with a smile when he realized its significance. He put the ring on the necklace, put the necklace around his neck, and then put it under his shirt.

"I have been saving it, hoping for this moment," Sabrina said.

"This is a very nice present! Thanks so much!"

And then, the unexpected happened. Detective Darnell Dupont strode into the bar.

Sabrina huffed. "How did you get so good at spoiling good moments! Nobody invited you!" she spat out.

Darnell replied, "I come in peace. May I sit?" Scott and Sabrina grudgingly nodded their assent. Joshua wondered what was going on. "I wanted to come in person to tell you some news. Do you remember when Johnny Dix got arrested?"

"Yeah," they said in unison.

"We found some things in his truck. Grass, tequila, and a gun."

"So?" Sabrina said impatiently.

"The gun was a .22 pistol." The trio's eyes widened at this news. "On a hunch, I had ballistics in Jackson test it. The results came a few days ago. The test was positive. That was the gun used to murder Dee Dee Scarborough."

"Whaaaaat!" Scott exclaimed.

"But you told me he had an alibi," Joshua said

"That's what we thought. But when those results came in, I went over to the plant where he worked and interviewed his two co-workers personally. The ones who were his alibi. They each stood by their story at first, until I asked them if they wanted to go to prison for accessory to murder. That sure changed their tunes."

"What did they say?" Joshua asked.

"They said they knew nothing about a murder. Johnny had asked them to cover for him so he could go buy some marijuana. He told them he would give each of them a bag if they would. And when he came back, he did as he said."

"So, Johnny has no alibi, and the murder weapon is his," said Sabrina.

"That's right," Darnell said. "So yesterday, we arrested him for the murder of his ex-wife. That was easy to do, since he was still in jail."

Breathing a deep and shaky sigh of relief, Sabrina asked, "So why did he do it?"

"He said that he was waiting for Dee Dee behind the bar that night to talk to her about seeing Haley. Apparently, she and Paul would not let him have any visitation."

"I don't blame them," Scott said.

"They had words, and Johnny, who was buzzed, said some nasty things, at which point Dee Dee spit in his face. Dix said he fired the pistol before he realized he had pulled it out. An act of rage. He is still trying to rationalize his behavior, because he regrets it so deeply. Truth be told, if he had been in his right mind, it probably wouldn't have happened. And if he had been in his right mind when he showed up here, he would've never been caught."

Anger had been boiling up within Sabrina, and she barked, "And all this time you have been harassing me, making my life miserable. We are even moving because of all this!"

"This may not mean much, Sabrina," the detective said. "But I am really, really sorry. I was just doing my job."

"And not very well, either! It took dumb luck for you to catch the murderer."

"You're right. You're right. I failed Criminal Investigation

101, so to speak. The first thing they teach us is don't form a theory too soon and fall in love with it. That's exactly what I did. You had motive and opportunity, so I couldn't see anything else, not really. I looked at Paul somewhat, but I didn't look close enough into Johnny Dix. I should have interviewed him and his co-workers myself, from the get-go. All I can say, again, is that I'm sorry."

Sabrina was mute, but Joshua asked, "What will become of Haley?"

"Paul and Johnny will both be going to prison, so hopefully, Johnny's parents will take her in. I just hope the state finds them fit to be her parents."

"Me, too," Joshua said with regret, thinking about his part in all of it.

"I want you to know one other thing," Darnell said. "This man sitting beside you is a true friend."

"What do you mean?" Sabrina asked, her demeanor softening.

"I'll let him fill in the details, but long story short, he put his life on the line trying to find the real killer. He always believed in you."

Scott and Sabrina stared at Joshua in surprise.

"Anyway, I need to run. I just hope that you have it in your heart someday to forgive me. Really and truly, I was just trying to do my job. Joshua, join me for a burger later?" Joshua nodded yes.

After he left, Joshua said, "Now you guys don't have to leave! Word will spread quickly about your innocence."

"It's too late for that," Sabrina said. "Like you, we need a fresh start."

"Then you can start by forgiving Darnell."

"Touche'!" Sabrina said and grinned. "But what did he mean about something you did?"

Joshua summed up his part in the story, including how convoluted his efforts became.

The couple was stunned. Scott said, "We will always

be grateful, man." After a pause, he continued, "You know, something just occurred to me. Maybe Dee Dee had a name written in water, like your Addie."

"Yes, I guess you're right," Joshua said. Then, as they rose to leave, he said farewell to his friends. "Like Greg said, I won't say goodbye. I will simply say 'until next time.'"

"Until next time," Sabrina and Scott said, giving Joshua one last hug.

Joshua felt a bit empty as he watched them leave the bar. He was no fan of farewells, especially with people he cared about. He wondered if he would see them again. And that reminded him of Addie. Would he ever see her again? Would he ever find out what happened to her? Could he ever forgive himself, like Miss Flo and Sabrina insisted?

He put these thoughts on hold, since he had to help close up. He restocked the beer cooler behind the bar and changed out a draft beer keg. He asked Jesse to clean the restrooms and Carly Jane to wipe down the bar and the tables. She also picked up the trash and carried it out. He was tallying up the amount of beer and liquor that had been consumed, when he heard someone come through the bar's door.

"Hello? Anyone home?" she asked.

Without looking, Joshua said, "Sorry, we're closed." Looking up, he saw a pretty, young woman with dark hair and dark eyes. With a start, Joshua realized who she was. It was Davy Crockett's vet, Leah West. Joshua touched the ring beneath his shirt and wondered what was next.

The End

ACKNOWLEDGEMENTS

Writing this book has been an interesting journey, full of stops and starts and twists and turns. It has been both exciting and challenging, especially since it is my first novel. Please be assured that I have no illusions about my abilities; however, I have come to understand that just because I can't write like F. Scott Fitzgerald doesn't mean I shouldn't write. So, I wrote for myself, the kind of book I like to read. If my family and friends read it and like it also, mission accomplished

I would like to thank some folks who helped along the way. For Tim and Toby, who answered my many questions about self-publishing, thanks friends. Thank you, Connie and Carol for reading my rough, rough drafts and giving me helpful hints concerning plot and character development. Thanks to my wife and daughters for encouraging me: Sharon, Melody, Rachel, Krista, and Katie. And, thanks to Katie for being my social media and promotions guru.

I hope you enjoyed the book. I look forward to completing and publishing its sequel: *The Secrets We Tell.* As Ben Franklin famously said, "Three may keep a secret if two of them are dead."

Someone will tell, and someone will die.

BOOK CLUB DISCUSSION QUESTIONS

1. What burden does Joshua carry? Is it justified?

2. What remedies does he seek to relieve his burden?

3. Why is he obsessed with solving Dee Dee's murder?

4. Who did you suspect was Dee Dee's murderer? Why? Did you suspect Joshua? Why or why not?

5. Describe the most intense or interesting part of the book for you. Why was it so?

6. Which character did you find most interesting? Why?

7. Music is a big part of this book, especially Delta Blues and 80's Country and Pop. What are your memories, associations, and thoughts about such music? How did its inclusion help you re-enter the world of that era?

8. Were you surprised by Darnell and Miss Flo's back story and history? If so, how? Did it seem realistic to you? Why or why not?

9. Were you surprised by Bubba Bryce's back story? If so, how? Did it seem realistic to you? Why or why not?

10. Why doesn't Joshua accept Miss Flo's invitation to the Christmas Eve service at her church?

11. What does Joshua mean by "the church of Jim

Beam"? Ever visited that church? (Rhetorical)

12. Discuss the themes of guilt and remorse as presented in the book. Do you have any experience with such feelings? (Don't tell it all, lol) How did you handle them?

13. What do you think of Miss Flo's advice about "laying down our burdens"?

14. Discuss the themes of self-forgiveness and redemption as presented in the book. Do you have any experience with such events? How did it change you?

15. What do you think really happened to Addie? Was Joshua involved? Why or why not?

16. Based on the ending of the novel, what do you think will happen next?